"Why the sudden interest in my brothers?"

Hannah shrugged. "You know all about my family. Maybe I want to know more about yours."

"Your family has always been in the spotlight," Will answered.

"All the more reason for me to know about yours."

"What do you want to know about me?"

Hannah reached up, sliding her fingertip between his brows.

"I want to know why these worry lines never seem to go away."

"Concerned for me?"

"More concerned for my career. I can't have you stressed when you're around me."

Her eyes dropped to his lips.

"And you think looking at me like you want to kiss me is keeping me calm?"

"Your ego is clouding your judgment. I don't want to kiss you."

Will smiled. "No?"

Hannah tipped her chin and smiled in invitation.

Then he covered her lips with his.

* * *

Twin Games in Music City by Jules Bennett is part of the Dynasties: Beaumont Bay series.

To Jessica Lemmon for the fun times in plotting, lake life, writer retreats where I invite myself to your house and all the laughs. I'm so thrilled to be doing this series with you.

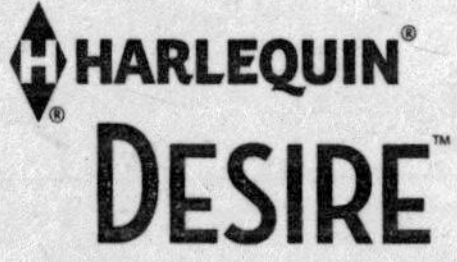

Recycling programs for this product may not exist in your area.

ISBN-13: 978-1-335-23285-4

Twin Games in Music City

This edition published by arrangement with Harlequin Books S.A.

For questions and comments about the quality of this book, please contact us at CustomerService@Harlequin.com.

Harlequin Enterprises ULC
22 Adelaide St. West, 40th Floor
Toronto, Ontario M5H 4E3, Canada
www.Harlequin.com

Printed in U.S.A.

DYNASTIES

Where family loyalties and passions collide.

Harlequin Desire brings you Dynasties—delicious, dramatic miniseries that span generations, include an engaging cast of characters and sweep you into the world of the American elite. From luxury ranch retreats to the stages of Nashville, from the sagas of powerful families to the redeeming power of passion... don't miss a single installment of Dynasties!

Dynasties: Beaumont Bay

What happens in Beaumont Bay stays in Beaumont Bay. This is the bedroom community where Nashville comes to play!

Twin Games in Music City by Jules Bennett
—available now
Second Chance Love Song by Jessica Lemmon
—available May 2021
Fake Engagement, Nashville Style by Jules Bennett
—available June 2021
Good Twin Gone Country by Jessica Lemmon
—available July 2021

Dynasties: The Carey Center

The Carey family works hard and plays harder as they build a performance space to rival Carnegie Hall!
From *USA TODAY* bestselling author Maureen Child
Available September, October, November and December 2021

Dynasties: The Ryders

For this perfect all-American family, image is everything. Until a DNA ancestry test reveals secrets they've hidden for generations...
From Joss Wood
Available February, March, April and May 2022

Dynasties: The Eddington Heirs

In Point du Sable, this empire is under siege. Only family unity and the power of love can save it!
From Zuri Day
Available July, August, September and October 2022

Dear Reader,

Welcome to Beaumont Bay, Tennessee—where the high rollers and celebrities come to play. This lakeside town has more than country music superstars. It has family drama, secrets, scandals and a hoity-toity, self-dubbed "first lady" of the Bay area.

Jessica Lemmon and I absolutely loved working on this series together, and you are getting a great start with book one! Hannah Banks is country music's sweetheart and the newest artist with Will Sutherland. They're planning on taking over the industry and making epic chart toppers. What they don't expect is the fling they're going to have to keep behind closed doors.

I've always loved a good twin story, and this one is no different! I couldn't just stop with the twins, though. I had to add in working together, a heated fling that can't leak to the press and, oh, did I mention Will has a whole host of hunky brothers? The Sutherland boys will be a huge part of this series and you are going to want to follow each of their stories!

Sit back, get cozy and welcome to Beaumont Bay!

Happy reading!

Jules

JULES BENNETT

TWIN GAMES IN MUSIC CITY

USA TODAY bestselling author **Jules Bennett** has published over sixty books and never tires of writing happy endings. Writing strong heroines and alpha heroes is Jules's favorite way to spend her workdays. Jules hosts weekly contests on her Facebook fan page and loves chatting with readers on Twitter, Facebook and via email through her website. Stay up-to-date by signing up for her newsletter at julesbennett.com.

Books by Jules Bennett

Harlequin Desire

The Rancher's Heirs

Twin Secrets
Claimed by the Rancher
Taming the Texan
A Texan for Christmas

Lockwood Lightning

An Unexpected Scandal
Scandalous Reunion
Scandalous Engagement

Dynasties: Beaumont Bay

Twin Games in Music City

Visit her Author Profile page at Harlequin.com, or julesbennett.com, for more titles.

You can also find Jules Bennett on Facebook, along with other Harlequin Desire authors, at Facebook.com/harlequindesireauthors!

One

Will Sutherland settled into the corner leather booth and watched as Hallie Banks wound her way through the tables at Rise and Grind.

This little meeting shouldn't already have him irritated, but it did. Will didn't want to meet with Hallie—he wanted to meet with her twin sister, Hannah.

But obviously, Hannah Banks, country superstar and America's sweetheart, couldn't be bothered with such mundane things as setting up her recording schedule for the next album or going over the tour dates and venues.

He'd only met her a handful of times in passing at various events within the industry. Will had always found her attractive; he'd have to be dead not to. Hannah Banks could make any man do a double take and he was no different.

As far as knowing her personally, he couldn't really say much, but this first official meeting wasn't going as planned.

Her selfish way of thinking might have worked for her old record label, but now that she'd signed with Elite, she was going to have to accept the very real fact that she wasn't in charge. He was.

Hallie offered a soft smile and reached to shake his hand. "Good morning. Have you been waiting long?"

Will came to his feet and gripped her hand, surprised by how soft and delicate she seemed. He didn't recall noticing Hallie's hands before…and he shouldn't be noticing them now.

He'd already found himself fantasizing about Hallie's sister, Hannah. The last thing he needed was an attraction to twins. That wouldn't be good for business, and being attracted to either of them didn't fit his professional style.

Hallie was more conservative in her wardrobe than her usual blinged-out sister. Perhaps that's because Hallie was the manager and worked behind the scenes in a quieter, calmer setting. Whereas Hannah was in-your-face, sparkly, over-the-top…and not at all the type of woman he should have been drawn to. Yet, he found himself noticing his new star more and more.

He needed to get his thoughts under control.

"I just got here myself." He gestured to the seat across from him. "Please, sit."

She put her bag in the vacant seat and settled into the chair with curved arms. A barista came right over to take their orders before leaving them alone again.

"So where did you say Hannah was and why couldn't she make it today?" he asked, hoping to get a direct answer this time.

Hallie blinked up at him. "Oh, I didn't say. She just asked me to meet you. After we talk, I will go over the schedule with her. She did request that she record in her home studio, so that was the main thing I'm supposed to tell you."

Of course. Will shouldn't have been surprised, though. Since that horrific storm had swept through Beaumont Bay only a few weeks ago, the town was still trying to recover. It was all hands on deck in this Nashville bedroom community to rebuild the multimillion-dollar homes that had taken a hit and the few businesses that had been affected.

The Bay wouldn't stay down long. This lakeside community was where Nashville came to play, where all the deals were done, where the country music elite hid their juiciest secrets. And it was a town that legendary music producer Mags Dumond pretty much owned…or thought she did.

He'd give Mags her due. She'd built up Beaumont Bay with her late husband and former mayor. It had been her foresight—and her insistence on hosting all her parties here over the decades—that had made a home, or second home, in the Bay a necessity for anyone who was anyone in Nashville.

Will's family had been born here, and not to a country music bloodline. Travis and Dana Sutherland were in the real estate industry and owned nearly everything…unless Mags had claim on it.

But the Sutherland brothers had made a name for themselves in the music industry by pulling themselves up by the bootstraps…and staying out of Mags's way for the most part. The woman had been a thorn in his family's side for decades, but he refused to think about that now. The next step in building his family's music empire was his new star, Hannah Banks, and finishing the renovations to the studio that had been damaged.

The reconstruction was taking much too long, although even a one-day delay was too long in this industry. He had music to make and singers relying on him, not to mention the trickle-down effect of the tours that were already being promoted to celebrate albums that were releasing soon.

The whole damn situation was a nightmare and Hannah Banks—the superstar he'd stolen from Mags, whom he needed to make this whole plan a reality—couldn't find the time for a courtesy, in-person meeting. Sending her sister/manager/twin wasn't the same.

"I would have to check out Hannah's recording studio before I could commit to that agreement," Will informed Hallie. "We are going to have to start the production process next week to keep up with the deadlines. Tell Hannah I'll be at her house first thing in the morning to check out this recording room of hers."

Hallie pursed her pale pink lips and shook her head. "Tomorrow morning won't work." She pulled out her phone and scrolled, then tapped her finger on the screen. "How about Tuesday at ten?"

Considering this was Friday, there was no way in hell he was waiting until Tuesday. Will pulled in a deep breath and sighed. Was Hallie going to be just as difficult as the country diva? The pout of her lips said yes, and something hard and dark moved inside him.

And that's when he knew something was off here.

"I'm not sure how things went when she worked for Mags at Cheating Hearts, but now that she's with Elite, I run the schedule and say when things are going to get done."

Hallie's eyes narrowed. "Is that right? Well, maybe I should've just stayed with Cheating Hearts."

Will inched forward, resting his hands on the table. "*Hannah?* Are you kidding me?"

She cursed beneath her breath and Will gritted his teeth. He'd known something felt off, but he'd never thought for a second his newest artist would play such a childish game as to pretend to be her twin. No way in hell would he fall for this swapped-twin trap.

Hannah Banks was about to learn who was in charge real quick.

* * *

Damn it. She hadn't meant to let that slip. How could she pretend to be her sister, even going so far as to dress like her and wear glasses, and yet not be able to simply hold her tongue?

Hannah squared her shoulders and stared across the table. Will Sutherland was so damn sexy, that's why. He had her so flustered she couldn't think.

All of this was his fault.

How could she keep up her disguise when all she could think about was raking her fingers through that hair to see if she could mess it up? Those lips, which were now thinned with frustration, seemed soft. Was he a good kisser?

She hadn't felt much of an attraction toward any man in a long time. Why did this man, of all the ones in her world, have to grab her attention? She'd hoped that pretending to be Hallie would tamp down some of the heat she felt whenever he was near.

No such luck and now she'd gone and blown her cover. As if she needed more problems.

She'd known switching record labels would be difficult, no matter which one she chose. Mags ruled this town and she hadn't wanted Hannah to move on. But Elite, and Will, were the best fit for where she wanted to go next. So she'd hoped she'd be able to ignore her attraction to one of the sexiest men in Beaumont Bay.

Apparently she'd have to do more than pose as

Hallie to keep her head on straight and focus on her career.

"What the hell game are you playing?" Will leaned forward and spoke through gritted teeth, pulling her from her thoughts.

Oh, those deep blue eyes got just a touch darker. Anger and arousal sometimes teetered on the very same thin line.

She clasped her hands together under the table, pushing aside her awareness. No way could she act on her desires. What would come of that? If Will returned her advances, then what? The media would eat them both alive and she'd be seen as getting this deal because she'd slept her way into it. All her work in establishing her new persona—and getting her own songs out into the world—would be for nothing.

No way in hell would she tarnish her reputation or that of Elite Records. Singing and performing were her entire life. She'd already risked nearly everything to leave Cheating Hearts for a chance at something new. She had nothing left to gamble on a fleeting attraction.

Besides, she'd chosen Elite because of their strong familial bond. Will and his three brothers were all in the music industry in one form or another. She knew having all of that surrounding the Elite name would help her in this new phase of her career.

"I'm not playing a game," she retorted with her sweetest tone.

"Then why the ruse?"

The barista interrupted them by setting down their drinks, then left them alone once again. Hannah reached for her chai tea with a splash of almond milk. Ah, yes. Perfect. A little touch of normalcy and familiarity in this tense moment was exactly what she needed to relax and feel more grounded.

"Hannah," Will commanded.

She met his gaze and shrugged as she curled her fingers around the mug. "I wanted to know more about what you were like as a person. Hallie met with you before, then we all signed papers, but I wanted a one-on-one in a relaxed setting to get you to know you without the pressure of you realizing who I really was."

He didn't say a word, but merely continued to stare with those striking eyes. A muscle clenched in his jaw. It was a strong jawline with a little dark shadowing of facial hair… Yum.

Calm down, Hannah. He can make or break your next career move.

If she wanted to be seen as something more than a young girl with cutesy songs, she needed Will. She needed this change. She wanted out of the rut that Mags had put her in, and the next chapter of her career hinged on getting everything right at this very time in her life. She couldn't afford mistakes if she wanted to go to the next level in the music industry and be seen as a serious songwriter.

"I don't know you very well." She forced herself to focus on the business and not the attraction that settled between them. "But I risked a great deal to come to your label. I wanted to know a little more about you as a person before I spoke to you as me."

"That makes no sense," he said. "And from here on out, there are no games."

"I'm not playing a game," she insisted again. "This is my career. I'm simply looking out for myself."

Hannah refused to let him into her head. She wasn't ready to share all the reasons behind her switch. All he'd been told was that Hannah hadn't been getting along with Mags and that's all he needed to know.

Mags and Hannah's grandmother went back decades, when they'd both first broken into the Nashville scene. Hannah's grandmother was the world-famous Eleanor Banks. The woman had sold more records in the country music industry than any other woman—move over Dolly.

No one could hold a candle to Eleanor's stardom and Mags was jealous. When Mags married, her husband was the mayor of Beaumont Bay and had dealings with real estate. He ended up buying her a record label to keep her happy and let her still have a hand in the industry. Her life intertwined with everybody's…and if it didn't, she'd place herself there.

Two generations later and Mags's jealousy was still in effect—it's why she'd wanted to sign Hannah nearly ten years ago.

Now after a decade of being ruled by Mags, Hannah wanted to break out of the twenty-something persona she'd been shoved into and delve into deeper, more emotional lyrics that really showcased her talent, ability, and creativity. She wanted to take her art and songwriting to the next level and reveal that she had more talents than just her voice. She truly believed she had something to share with her lyrics.

So she'd signed with Will and had agreed to the conditions that she'd record a song written by Cash Sutherland—one of Will's brothers—and that his brother would be her opening act for her new tour. Cash had that bit of a bad boy reputation and Will was convinced having the two team up would only help Cash's image with his climb to stardom.

"We will record at my house," she went on, keeping her tone firm. She'd learned from Mags that she had to be firm to get her way, so she was laying down the groundwork now that she wouldn't be bossed or bullied. This move to Elite Records was her chance to make her own way and for once she would be in charge.

"You can come look and judge all you want," she continued, "but that's the best place. I'm comfortable there and everything is state-of-the-art. You won't find better equipment anywhere else."

Will shrugged. "We'll see. Once my studio is restored, we will be working from there. I trust you looked over Cash's song? The one that I sent through your sister?"

Hannah nodded. "I wanted to talk to you about

that. I'm not sure that's the first song we should release as a single."

Considering she wanted to start over with a brand-new sound, she didn't want to rely on someone else's lyrics right away. She had her own lyrics, several songs actually, but she'd kept them locked away as a secret. Even her sister didn't know those pieces existed.

She'd hoped to present them to Will and see if they could make this launch new in every way. Up until now, she'd always recorded other people's songs. She really wanted her own to be on her first album with Elite.

"Cash's song was written into the contract," Will replied, as if she didn't know that legal agreement forward and backward. "Nonnegotiable."

The way he delivered that final word coupled with his intense stare had her feeling…way too much. She didn't want to find his dominance sexy. She wanted to get to work and be taken seriously as a singer-songwriter. But, in order for the songwriter part to happen, she would have to open herself up.

Not quite yet, but soon.

The idea both terrified and excited her. She'd never exposed herself like this before. Singing words from someone else's mind was one thing, but letting her fans in on her own private thoughts was entirely another.

Even though she was Hannah Banks, five-time winner of the female artist award and vocalist of the year for the past six years, she still had insecurities. Rejection was always a fear and could be a detrimental roadblock if she didn't scrounge up some courage soon. She'd made the leap to Elite; she'd find the courage to ultimately take that final step.

"I'll need to come by and see your house," he stated, cutting into her thoughts.

"When?"

His long fingers curled around his mug and she couldn't help but stare. Everything about him screamed power, sex appeal, and too many other equally alluring—and frustrating—qualities to count. There was risk here—a risk she refused to take. It took every ounce of her willpower to remember she needed to shut down any hint of attraction. Will and Elite would take her to the next level of her career…and nothing more.

"Since tomorrow doesn't work, we'll go now."

Hannah laughed. "Now? That's not possible."

"Fine," he growled. "In an hour."

Hannah sighed and shook her head. "That's not much different than now."

Will eased aside his mug as he leaned toward her. "I'm not sure of how you handled your working relationship with Mags, but with me, I'm hands-on, and I will be with you each and every step of this process. My name is associated with this label as well, so I won't let even one slipup happen."

"Do you think I want something to go wrong?" she asked, barely containing a sneer. "This is my career. I'm taking a huge leap leaving Mags to sign with another label and letting your brother open for my upcoming tour."

"Excuse me."

Hannah glanced up to see a young teenage girl wearing a nervous grin.

"I'm sorry," the girl stated. "But you're like my favorite singer and would you mind giving me an autograph?"

Hannah never tired of meeting fans and giving autographs. This was a part of the business she absolutely loved. She remembered how sweet her grandmother had always been with the public. Gram had always said without the fans, there would be no music business. So Hannah was grateful for each and every autograph and photo with the people who bought her music and kept her in the industry she so loved.

"I don't mind a bit," Hannah replied with a smile. "Do you have something to write on?"

The girl's face fell as she reached for her little cross-body purse and started searching.

"Here." Will grabbed a clean napkin from the stack and pulled a pen from his pocket. "Will this work?"

"Perfect." Hannah slid the items across and glanced back to the girl. "What's your name?"

"Tasha. I listen to your music every day when I'm practicing dance. It really helped me escape since my parents separated."

Hannah signed the napkin, using her familiar heart signature. Everyone who asked for an autograph always told her how her music affected them and she loved every story. Affecting people's lives in a positive way—that's what she wanted. She loved hearing how she'd helped someone get through a difficult time, no matter what it might be.

"I'm so sorry about your parents," Hannah replied as she handed Tasha the napkin. "I'm glad I can comfort you in some small way."

Tasha looked to the autograph, her beaming smile returning. "This is so cool. Wait until I show my friends. Thank you so much."

Hannah pushed back her chair and came to her feet. She held out her arms and embraced the young girl.

"It was my pleasure, Tasha. I'm so glad I could meet you."

The teen practically skipped back to the counter where she retrieved her drink and headed out the front door. Hannah sank back down into her seat and scooted toward the table.

She stilled when she caught Will's gaze studying her.

"What?"

"It's not every superstar who would let a meeting or a coffee date be interrupted for an autograph."

"First of all, this is not a date." Good grief. It was as if he'd gotten a glimpse into those unwanted thoughts she'd been hiding. "Second of all, if you're offended because I interrupted our little meeting, then get used to it. If it weren't for my fans, I wouldn't have a career and you wouldn't have money coming in from me."

Will's lips quirked into a grin and she realized he could be both frustrating and sexy at the same time… Well, *that* would equal nothing but trouble.

"I wasn't complaining about the interruption," he explained. "You should always talk to your fans. All I said was it's not just anyone who would do that."

Flustered and still turned on from his arousing good looks and take-control attitude, Hannah huffed and turned in her seat to cross her legs. If she hadn't slipped up, she could still be pretending to be Hallie and then she wouldn't have to worry about anything. Hallie was calm, quiet and determined, but in a controlled way. Hannah too often felt like her emotions were out of control, like she'd lost herself somewhere during all those years when she'd let Mags determine her public persona. She was still trying to find herself.

Which was why she needed to focus on this pivotal point in her life and career.

"I don't want to argue," she told him. "So if you want to come to my house, let's go. I have other things to do today."

Things that were none of his business and things that she didn't want to share. She might be in every magazine and splattered all over the internet, but she still wanted to keep her insecurities to herself. While she loved the life she'd created, she also still valued her privacy. And just because Will owned her music now didn't mean that he owned her as a person.

Trying to prove to her fans and the public that she wasn't the diva Mags had portrayed her as would take some work, too. But Will didn't know her or her working style and there was only one first impression to make.

Annoyingly, Hannah also had to keep reminding herself that they were only working together… nothing more. Which meant she couldn't want him or even flirt with him. This next chapter of her life had to be completely aboveboard professionally so she could start showcasing herself as an adult performer and a serious songwriter.

Just because she hadn't been turned on by a man in longer than she could count did not mean she should act on her attraction now.

Hannah's desires would have to just go away because she refused to risk it all for a one-time, but surely delicious, romp in the sack with Will Sutherland.

Two

It wasn't often that he was surprised, but when Will glanced around the state-of-the-art studio he could barely contain his shock. He hadn't expected Hannah to have so much technology and space in her home. He'd just assumed she'd be the type to let everyone else do the heavy lifting, so to speak, and just use others' studios. But knowing she was this involved in the smallest details of her career was actually refreshing…and a bit of a turn-on.

Though he really shouldn't be shocked, not when her grandmother was Eleanor Banks. No doubt perfection and high standards had been the norm for Hannah from a young age.

Still, with her reputation of being a diva and always having her hair, makeup, and clothes perfectly placed, he was pleasantly surprised that she didn't just put on the façade, but she also dug deeper to work her career.

"This will do."

Hannah laughed. "Wow, hold off on all the compliments."

He faced her and again ignored that ping of arousal. She'd changed her clothes since they'd been at the coffee shop. Now she wore a pair of black fitted jeans that sat so low they should be illegal. She'd paired those with a sparkly blue top that didn't meet the top of her pants, leaving a good two inches of creamy skin exposed. She'd even added more makeup and done something with her hair to make it…hell, he didn't know. Bigger?

How did she go from small-town Hannah to stage-ready Hannah in such a short time? Was she always like this at home? A superstar even in her own surroundings? Couldn't she just be herself? Or maybe she'd been molded into this persona for so long, she'd lost herself along the way.

Hell, he wasn't sure and he didn't need to know. That was an emotional level he never needed to get in to with her. So long as she continued to crank out hits, as she'd been doing, that's all he cared about.

Well, he also cared about the state of his studio at the moment.

When they'd left the coffee shop, he had stopped by Elite to check on the renovations. They weren't getting done fast enough to suit him, but since construction wasn't in his wheelhouse, there wasn't much he could do besides wait. And for now, they could use Hannah's studio.

"I'd like Cash here when we record 'Kiss My Heart,'" he told her. "It's only fair since it's his song and the two of you will be touring together."

He watched a variety of expressions float across her face, too fast for him to fully name, but he didn't need to know how she felt. He wasn't here to get personal; he was here to make money and Hannah Banks was the ticket to helping Elite and helping his brother clean up his reputation.

"Fine," she told him. "Do you need him to record here, too? We have the other song we were going to do as a duet."

Will shook his head. "We should be good for everything other than that one. He recorded quite a bit before the storm came through. He has a couple songs to voice over, but he can do that at his own place. We'll definitely do the duet here since my studio won't be finished for almost three more weeks."

It still seemed like a lifetime to him. Hannah and Cash weren't the only talents at his label, so he needed to get back to work to make up for the lost time. Not having control over his own space was definitely putting him out of his comfort zone.

Being at the mercy of Hannah and in her territory was sure as hell not making him comfortable. The place smelled like her. All floral and sexy. Her studio was quite a bit more feminine than his. She had a soft yellow rug on the floor of the recording area. There were a few photos on the wall of her grandmother on the stage at various shows. No doubt Eleanor Banks had been a motivation and support for Hannah.

Eleanor had moved to the Bay area some years back. She had a massive, three-story home back up in the mountains for privacy. She still appeared on awards shows or produced duets with up and coming stars on occasion. She was, and always would be, an icon.

He hoped like hell Hannah was this generation's Eleanor Banks.

"Cash is more than welcome to record here," Hannah stated, cutting in to his unwanted thoughts. "I've really only met him in passing at awards shows. We might as well get to know each other since we'll be together for months next summer."

Will nodded. "I'll make that happen. Monday work for you?"

She pursed her bright pink lips as she thought and Will's entire body stirred at the sight. He was in trouble with this one...and not the trouble that had to do with music. Damn, he hadn't realized when he'd signed her that she would affect him in such a sexual manner. He figured he'd have to deal with a little bit of a diva, but he hadn't once thought about being attracted to her.

The country music world was flooded with gorgeous women, from artists to industry professionals. Why was he attracted to Hannah? Why did this woman—who was likely going to irritate the hell out of him as they worked together—drive him crazy with want?

Probably because he couldn't have her.

Will Sutherland always got what he wanted, when he wanted. If there wasn't a way to obtain his desires immediately, he eventually found a way to make it happen, anyway.

Having Hannah in a personal, intimate capacity would sure as hell not be happening. He'd invested too much in her professionally. And the thought that he couldn't have what he wanted made him a tad irritated.

"I can't do Monday morning. I have an important personal appointment," she told him. "I can be back here by two if that's good."

"I have a meeting that afternoon with my contractor."

"Send Cash, anyway," she suggested with a shrug. "We don't need you here necessarily."

Like hell they didn't need him here, as a chaperone if nothing else. Uncharacteristic jealousy flooded through him. There was no way Will could unleash his flirty, playboy brother onto Hannah. The last thing any of them needed was a heated fling to stir up the press. The focus was Hannah's relaunch and establishing Cash's new squeaky clean reputation.

Which was exactly what Will had to say to himself, as well. Hannah was off-limits…to all Sutherlands.

The Sutherland brothers were all single and successful. With Cash a country music artist, Gavin an attorney to the stars, and Luke owning several upscale bars and restaurants in the area that catered to celebrity appearances, they were each probably appealing to an available woman. But not Hannah. No way in hell could she get personally entangled with any of them.

"I'll rework my schedule," he told her. "Monday afternoon will work."

She narrowed her eyes and took a step toward him. "You don't trust Cash and me to get along without you? I promise I'll play nice."

Hannah offered him a megawatt smile that shot straight to the part of his anatomy that had no place in this business meeting.

"Nobody will be playing anything," he informed her, trying to circle back around to being the professional, music-label owner that he was.

She cocked her head, clearly trying to be flirty or adorable—he wasn't sure which, but he had no interest in figuring it out. He had a feeling she knew just how well she could get under his skin.

"Oh, I'm sure we can make time for something fun," she suggested. "You know what they say about all work and no play."

"Yeah. All work means a bigger bank account."

Hannah rolled her eyes. “Money, money, money. You sound like Mags.”

Will reacted before he could think, carefully curling his fingers around her elbow. “Don’t ever compare me to that woman again,” he demanded as her bright eyes widened. “She’s nothing like me.”

Before he even realized what he intended, he gave her a gentle tug until she fell against his chest. His hold wasn’t tight, but he still hadn’t meant to touch her at all. Touching would only fuel that desire for what he couldn’t have…desire that was essentially forbidden.

Hannah’s lips parted as her gaze went to his mouth, then back to his eyes. Every part of his body tightened and that’s when he realized his mistake. Too late. Somehow he’d lost control of himself—something he never did.

Hannah’s hands flattened against his chest as she continued to stare up at him and Will quickly realized their bodies were plastered together and her perfect pink lips were still parted. That gaze moved to his mouth once again and Will released her before he was burned by the fire that he’d ignited.

“Not a Mags Dumond fan?” Hannah crossed her arms over her chest, seemingly unphased by their encounter. “The feeling is mutual. She sees you as a threat.”

“I am.”

Hannah’s mouth quirked into a crooked smile that only made her look adorable even as she was trying to be saucy. "She's also feeling the pressure now that I left her label. She'll try for Cash."

Will busted out laughing. "She'd have to have big balls to go after my brother."

"Oh, they're big," Hannah replied with a soft laugh. "She goes after anything she wants and nobody is off-limits."

"Every single Elite artist is off-limits," Will growled. "Especially you and Cash. I hope she approaches him. He'll laugh in her face and tell her exactly what he thinks of her offer."

"Are your brothers all like you?" she asked.

Will jerked slightly. "Like me? How?"

Hannah shrugged. "Outspoken, determined, arrogant."

Will couldn't help but laugh at her once again. "Thank you for the compliments."

"Of course, you would take all of that as a compliment," she muttered.

Will slid his hands into his pockets. "Are we going to continue to butt heads?"

"I'm easy to get along with usually. I mean, Mags and I clashed, because I always felt like she was trying to control me, to live her life through me…if that makes sense."

Oh, that made perfect sense. Margaret Dumond had wanted to be the next big thing in country music when she'd been younger. She'd been overshadowed by Hannah's grandmother, Eleanor. The two had debuted at the same time, but the fans had clicked with Eleanor.

Then Mags married Edward Prescott the mayor of Beaumont Bay, even then a monied bedroom community of Nashville. Her family had been founding members of Beaumont Bay decades ago, which was why she still clung to her maiden name of Dumond.

Edward had absolutely adored the woman. He'd bought her a record label and thus Cheating Hearts was born. Clearly Mags knew that if she wanted to make a name for herself in the industry, it wouldn't come from her singing.

Once she had the label and a few artists beneath her belt, she had the power, reputation, and ego to bring Nashville's superstars to Beaumont Bay. She'd dubbed herself "The First Lady of Beaumont Bay," and the industry had played along.

"I'm easy to get along with, as well," he informed Hannah, picking up their conversation. "Providing you do what I say and we don't have any more of those twin-swapping games."

Hannah rolled her eyes. "You really need to get over that switch. You're too cute to be so surly."

Cute? What was he, a puppy?

"Flirting will get you nowhere with me."

She cocked her head and flashed that smile that stirred his desire even more. Damn it. She knew how powerful her sex appeal was, but he wasn't going to be another man who fell for it. Hannah Banks could have any guy she wanted...except him. All he wanted from her was epic sales and her help in boosting his brother to stardom.

"Honey, if you think I'm flirting, you've been hanging around the wrong women."

Why did that Southern drawl come across as tempting as fiery bourbon?

And he hadn't been hanging around any women outside of work. Will had been devoting all his energy into keeping Elite the top record label since he'd taken over when he was only twenty-seven. With his parents in real estate, catering to million-dollar mansions and commercial properties, Will had gotten a bargain on the location and had used his wise investments to get the startup funds.

Will loved everything about the industry—growing up in Beaumont Bay made it easy to fall in love with country music. Nashville had nothing on this lakeside community. This was where the heavy hitters came to play, to get away from the crowds, to live a slow, easy, posh lifestyle. It's where they came to be themselves, to unwind at the local bars, to get back to their roots and play music for fun without the constrictions of contracts.

Will didn't live far from Hannah, but he'd never been to her home before. They'd only met once briefly, in his studio just before the storm hit. Then he'd met with her manager and sister, Hallie, at his house for most of the discussions and negotiations. And during those meetings with Hannah's twin, he'd never felt the desire he felt with Hannah. Not once.

What Hannah was doing to him was totally uncharted territory.

If Hannah was getting flirty with him, then she would try to get flirty with Cash, no doubt. Will loved his brothers, but Cash and Gavin were known to be ladies' men and they made no apologies about their lifestyle. None of the Sutherland men did, but Will and Luke were a tad calmer. They worked hard and played equally as hard…which was what made them so damn dynamic and successful.

"Who I do or don't hang around with in my personal time really isn't your concern," he countered.

"It might not be my concern, but the press does love to snap photos of both of us, and I'm here to tell you, that woman you took to dinner a couple of weeks ago is not nice."

Will couldn't help but laugh. "Not nice? What are we? In elementary school?"

"I was raised to speak my mind, but I do still have Southern manners. I'm keeping my real adjectives in my head."

Intrigued, Will crossed his arms, very interested in hearing exactly what Hannah thought of his date with Bethany. He had been completely bored out of his mind, but he was keeping that bit of information to himself. She'd been his first date in months, and from the silence on Bethany's end, she hadn't been looking for a second date, either.

"Just trust me when I tell you she's a bit of a gossip," Hannah went on. "She used to work for an online tabloid, so I'm sure she was just out for some fodder."

Only slightly offended, he dropped his arms and took a step toward her until she had to tip her head back to look him in the eye. Why did he keep getting so close? Why was he torturing himself with such temptation?

He'd never been denied anything, so maybe what he was feeling here was just the thrill of the challenge. Whatever it was, there was something about Hannah that made him want to uncover her layers, find the woman who lived beneath the surface of what the public saw.

"Are you saying she wasn't out with me for my stellar charm and good looks?" he asked, barely suppressing a smile.

Hannah patted his cheek. "Don't let my comment hurt your feelings. I'm sure she found you cute in that surly sort of way, but I promise, she's trying to get in with a magazine as a new gossip columnist… or so I was told."

"That's ironic."

Hannah's smile spread. "A little."

That smile and those eyes…and damn it, everything about her was getting to him when he'd sworn he wouldn't let her get under his skin. She'd been just as beautiful in the coffee shop without all the makeup or her hair teased or bling on her shirt. Maybe he should've stipulated in her contract that she should just be herself in private.

Regardless, he wasn't digging too deep into this. He hadn't signed on to be her therapist. He was just going to have to ignore that pull of lust and be a professional…you know, the way he was with every other star he represented.

Will took a step back, surprised when she seemed a little disappointed. That smile faltered and her shoulders sank just a touch. If he hadn't been staring like a damn fool, he would've missed it.

If this attraction went both ways, they were heading down a path toward nothing but disaster. What would an affair between them look like to the public? That Hannah had swapped labels after he seduced her? No way in hell would he tarnish her name, or his, in such a manner.

"I'll be back Monday with Cash," he told her, ready to remove himself from this situation. "Two o'clock."

He didn't wait for her to argue or start flirting again. The more he was around her, the more he had to remind himself she was not available for anything personal.

Elite had a reputation for producing some of the best music in the industry and having Hannah in his queue was going to skyrocket his label into even bigger territories. This would be from old school Opry to present-day country. The world loved Hannah Banks. He was even thinking of expanding her tour dates to do something international.

Will turned from the studio and showed himself

out before he made a mistake and touched her…or, worse, found out what her lips tasted like. Keeping his thoughts on how to grow her brand, how to market her new sound—that was what he needed to focus on. Because Cash was also involved in this and if Will and Hannah crossed that invisible line, Cash would also suffer.

There was too much pressure on Will. All eyes were on him, his label, his family, and Hannah. So there would be no touching and no kissing—no nothing that didn't involve music. Hell, maybe *he* needed a chaperone when he met with her from now on.

Was it too early to hit up one of Luke's bars for a drink?

Three

Will curled his hand around his cold mug and relaxed into the cushioned chair along the glass wall of Luke's rooftop bar. Cheshire was always hopping and crowded, but after hours, as in two in the morning, there was a nice calmness to the place, and he and his brothers could decompress and chill.

After his in-person encounter with Hannah yesterday, Will desperately needed to take a mental break with a locally brewed craft beer.

"Why are you scowling?"

Will glanced to his other brother, Gavin, who was sitting across from him and holding his own mug. Gavin had crazy, messy hair that he always seemed to be running his fingers through, but somehow that shaggy look worked for him. He was the best damn attorney Will knew, which was why Gavin was on retainer for Elite Records.

"I'm not scowling," Will replied. "I'm enjoying the peace and quiet."

Honking and laughter filtered up from below, totally contradicting his statement. He took a long pull of his beer and wondered why he hadn't tried a sample of this one before he decided on a tall glass. Definitely not his favorite.

Cheshire was one of the most popular bars in town, which made sense considering it was on top of the poshest hotel, The Beaumont. They had a very distinct clientele, but Cheshire welcomed everyone—from the rich and famous to the wannabe rich and famous. Luke opened up all his bars to anyone looking for a good time.

"You've been scowling since you got here," Luke chimed in as he came over with his own drink. "Work or woman issues?"

Both…which had never happened before and that's what pissed him off. He'd never crossed those two lines and he sure as hell didn't intend to start now. He prided himself on being professional and Hannah Banks was not going to be his downfall.

"Hannah Banks."

That's all he said when his brother Cash groaned.

"She's a diva, isn't she?" Cash asked, standing behind Will's chair with his beer. "She's sexy and can sing flawlessly, but what am I going to have to work with?"

Will shook his head. “You’ll be fine. She’s just… frustrating.”

Luke laughed and eased forward in his seat. “You work in the music industry. Everything and everyone is frustrating.”

Not like Hannah. She had already gotten in his head and wiggled her way into a spot where he didn’t want her. He’d dreamed about her last night and found himself replaying that damn erotic scene over and over all day. Now he was sexually frustrated and had nobody to blame but himself.

Damn woman had too much power over him already and they hadn’t even fully started working together.

“We still going Monday?” Cash asked. “I’m anxious to start working with her.”

Work, yes. That’s all he should be focused on. Getting Hannah a jump start with Elite and cementing Cash’s reputation in the entertainment world were his purposes right now. His other recording artists were climbing the charts and thankfully nobody needed a recording session before those renovations were due to be completed.

Damn high-wind storm. His home had been spared, thankfully, but a portion of the studio hadn’t been so lucky. The damage had given him the opportunity to do some remodeling and updates in the lobby that he’d been wanting to do but had kept putting off.

"We're going," Will told Cash. "Her recording studio is top-notch. I was impressed."

"That's saying something," Gavin replied. "You're a snob."

Will took another drink and sighed. "I'm not a snob. I refuse to settle for less than perfection when it comes to my work. There's a big difference."

But he knew there was a nugget of truth in what his brother was saying. He aimed for perfection with anything in his life—professionally or personally. Maybe that's why he'd never settled down…not that he was looking to. If it happened, it happened. But Elite was definitely more than a full-time job, especially when having so many artists kept him very busy when they had personal crises. He hardly ever thought about how he came home to a lonely house at night. He'd built a vast, three-story home on the lake. Eight bedrooms, ten baths, two kitchens, and more living space than he would ever need.

But in that house, alone, Will was in control of his own fate. He had to be. At twenty, he'd been fired from a Nashville label after making an honest mistake. Since that day, he'd refused to fail at anything or let anyone else control his future.

That went for everything in his life—business and personal.

His brothers were all bachelors, too, and if one of them married off or got a serious girlfriend, she'd have to fit in with this tight crew. Luke had been engaged once, but that had fallen apart and Luke never talked about her anymore. Their mother would love nothing more than for all of them to settle down and start producing little Sutherland babies.

"I'm anxious to hear Hannah sing my song," Cash stated. "When I wrote it, I knew a woman had to perform it and her tone and presence is perfect for those lyrics."

Will could practically hear Hannah's voice with Cash's song. It would be magical and, no doubt, award-winning, and he just knew when the time came to hear the final result there would be another sucker punch of lust to his gut.

He couldn't go into their next meeting distracted by thoughts worthy of an adolescent schoolboy. He was the music producer of a multimillion-dollar label with legendary recording artists. They all demanded the best and that's exactly what he provided. Hannah hadn't left Mags just to come to his label and start a fling. Good grief, he was an idiot for letting any inappropriate thoughts creep in.

There didn't seem to be anything he could do to turn them off, though. He was doomed to sexual frustration until he got his hormones under control. What he needed was to go on a date, maybe hook up with someone. Anything to get Hannah out of his mind and out of his system.

"Are you guys opening your tour in Beaumont Bay?" Luke asked. "Because I know of a place."

Will laughed. "I was going to discuss that with you, actually."

"Which bar?" Cash asked.

Luke owned several high-end bars around the area and all of them were equally popular, but Will had always preferred Cheshire to have a few beers.

Will glanced around to the open space with a long bar on one end and the stage and dance floor on the other. In the middle were low, fat ottomans for seating and an occasional high table for standing and mingling.

"This one," Luke replied. "I have VIP guests that would love an exclusive. I do them a few times a year, but I never announce who the performer is going to be. Hannah sang here once, years ago, but there's nobody I'd rather have than my own brother up on that stage."

Cash smiled and Will swelled with pride for his younger brother. A rogue reputation would only go so far. There was a great deal to be said about a southern gentleman and that's the new angle Will needed his brother to go. His voice was something the industry hadn't experienced in a long, long time. Now he needed the smooth persona to go with the musical tone.

The four Sutherland brothers might have taken different directions with their lives, but they were always there for each other. There was no greater support system. Their careers were all intertwined, and their strengths complemented each other's, which was just another way they could be connected and loyal to one another.

"Why hasn't Hannah been back to perform here?"

Luke shook his head. "I tried to get her a couple times, but just ended up butting heads with Mags. That woman is exhausting and I didn't want to deal with her flirting."

Will nearly choked on his beer. "She flirted with you?"

Gavin and Cash both laughed, but Luke wasn't amused, if his drawn eyebrows and thinned lips were any indication. Mags was quite a handful—in Beaumont Bay, in Nashville, in the industry—and Will couldn't imagine her sinking her flirty claws into someone.

"Nothing about that woman is amusing," Luke growled. "She undresses me with her eyes."

"She doesn't care who she flirts with," Gavin stated. "She legitimately believes everyone adores her simply because her family founded Beaumont Bay and she's the only one left with the Dumond name."

"I don't believe that's what she thinks," Will retorted. "She's obscenely arrogant, though, so who knows."

Will didn't want to deal with that woman any more than he had to. She drove around in her big white SUV like she owned the town…and in some ways she did. She was the "First Lady," thanks to her husband, but Cheating Hearts Records was Mags's baby. She was all too quick to flash her money around…and her power. She hadn't made it as a big star back in the day and so she tried to make up for it by ruling her town, and her artists' careers, in the manner *she* wished.

Will preferred to provide guidance to his artists, and discuss matters, rather than dictate. He liked to control the details of his business, but when it came to an artist's career, he had no place for that. He let his artists' sales and their awards speak for his label. There was no need to be arrogant about his status as a star maker.

He finished his beer and sat the mug on the table then got to his feet. "I need to head home."

"Why?" Luke asked. "Nothing for you at home."

"I have an early call with a client who's traveling overseas," he explained, then turned to Cash. "I'll meet you at Hannah's on Monday. Park outside the gate and I'll get you inside."

Cash nodded. "I'll be there."

"Are we all invited?" Luke asked.

Gavin chuckled. "I'm busy, but another time."

Will shook his head. "I'm not inviting everyone to her house. You all can see her when she plays here."

Gavin rolled his eyes. "You're trying to keep her for yourself."

No way in hell would Will admit he didn't want Hannah around his very eligible brothers. She'd bat those eyelashes and have one, or all of them, falling at her feet.

It was absolutely absurd the way his thoughts kept betraying his common sense. Jealousy wasn't something he was familiar with and he sure as hell didn't like it rearing its ugly head in this situation.

"Trust me," Will replied. "I'm not getting involved with Hannah Banks. She's going to be a handful in a professional capacity. I can't imagine how difficult she is personally. Besides, romantic relationships in this industry rarely last."

He'd seen it time and time again. New artists fell in love with seasoned singers and it was all love songs and sold-out tours and the next thing he knew they were making headlines about splitting up—which spawned their next chart-topper. He really didn't want to make headlines for anything other than being the best damn producer in the industry.

Will said goodbye to his brothers and left them to their drinks and gossip as he made his way to the private elevator. He loved getting together with them, but right now he really just wanted a few good hours of sleep. Maybe tonight he wouldn't dream of a petite vixen who could sing like a saint and undress him with her eyes like a sinner.

The heart knows... The heart...

Hannah groaned.

The lyrics were not coming out right. They seemed like a great idea in her head, but by the time she started singing and wrote them down, they were falling flat, sounding almost juvenile, which was the exact opposite of what she wanted.

Sitting on the floor of her studio, Hannah glanced

at her notes and tore out the sheet. After she crumpled the paper into a ball and tossed it, she adjusted her guitar strap and tried again. She played a couple of chords, then jotted down more lyrics.

There were days when her creative spirit just soared, but other days, like today, she just couldn't clear her thoughts to get through to the music.

She blamed her hot new music producer, Will Sutherland, for that. Her muddled mind was all his fault.

She'd been too attracted too fast. Her thoughts were too out of control. Sexy, powerful men weren't a rare commodity around Beaumont Bay. There were beautiful people everywhere. But Will did something to her she hadn't felt for a long, long time.

None of that mattered.

Her wants and desires outside of her career had to be put on hold. She needed to make this change work. Swapping labels was a very big deal and she wanted to be taken seriously. So why the hell did she think she could flirt with him? She wasn't that twenty-something singer who smiled and expected all the doors to open anymore. No, now she was an independent woman who knew the good and bad of this industry, who wanted to make it to the next level with her own music and her own style.

While her contract did mention she would have more say over the music she performed, she still hadn't talked to Will about her own pieces. She had an entire journal full of songs, but she wanted something perfect, something timeless, to take to him first. Her head wasn't in the right space now.

Will and Cash were coming over in just a bit and she still had to get ready. There were times she could dress in a more low-key way, like her twin, Hallie, but Hannah always felt people expected her to look a certain way.

She set aside her guitar and got to her feet. After putting everything away, she took her notebook and headed to her en suite bedroom. She put the notes on her nightstand, where she always kept them when she wasn't working. Oftentimes, when she couldn't sleep, she'd reach for the pen and paper to help her relax.

As she searched through her walk-in closet, Hannah wasn't quite sure what to wear for her first official meeting with Cash Sutherland. Oh, she'd seen him at various awards shows and around town, but nothing like this. Now that they were with the same label, working on a duet, they'd be together quite a bit, not to mention the big tour they had coming up.

Cash was definitely an up-and-coming star, having already won a few awards, and she had no doubt her fans would love him, too. He'd just gotten a little bit too rowdy at prior shows and maybe had been a tad outspoken with the media.

But, he had those devilish good looks and a charming smile, and that voice of his could make anyone turn up their radio and tap their foot. And he was just at the right age where moms and their teen daughters could easily agree that he was smokin' hot.

But it wasn't Cash that Hannah found herself wanting to impress. For reasons she refused to admit, she wanted Will to be taken with her. She liked that quiet power of his.

It was wrong, all of these fiery emotions stirring and bubbling within her, but she couldn't help herself.

Hannah grabbed a red halter jumpsuit and smiled as she changed and settled down to her vanity to complete her superstar look.

If she happened to catch Will's eye, just for today, well, that wouldn't be such a bad thing...would it?

Four

Will nearly choked on his own breath when Hannah opened the door.

He didn't need to look over to his brother to know Cash was also enjoying the unexpected, tantalizing view.

Who knew red was Will's favorite color? And who knew Hannah would appear so striking and glittery in her own home?

"Come on in," Hannah greeted with a wide smile. Her lips matched that damn body-hugging outfit. "I'm so glad to finally meet you in a more private, personal setting, Cash."

Will watched as his brother shook hands with Hannah. He was clearly intrigued by his new tour partner. On-stage chemistry was always a crowd pleaser, but Will wasn't looking for them to do anything other than make great music together. That was it.

"Pleasure is all mine, ma'am." Cash nodded.

"Call me Hannah." She offered Cash a wide smile that had Will gritting his teeth. "Let's head to the studio. Can I get you guys anything to drink first?"

"We're fine," Will answered. "Let's get started."

Hannah glanced to Cash. "Is he always this cranky?"

"He's always all business," Cash replied with a chuckle. "You'll get used to it."

Will refused to be baited by his brother and the woman who was a walking fantasy come to life. The sooner he could get his head on straight, the sooner they could make this recording and start pulling in money. The buzz around Hannah swapping labels already had sales spiking, but those sales were all going to Mags for previous hits.

Will and Cash followed Hannah up the steps and Will refused to stare at her ass. The urge to do so was childish, unprofessional. He had more respect for her than that.

It was hard to keep his eyes away, though.

As she led them into the studio, Cash let out a whistle as he circled the sound room.

"Damn, this is amazing."

Hannah beamed with pride, as she should have. "Thank you. My grandmother taught me everything I know."

"She may have taught you all about sound equipment and the industry, but your voice is all your own," Cash told her.

As much as he was right, Will didn't want his brother complimenting Hannah and flirting with her. Will refused to consider he was jealous—he wasn't. There was no room or time for that unwanted emotion in this business deal.

"That's sweet of you to say."

Hannah's accent seemed thicker when she was smiling and batting her lashes. The woman knew how to turn on the charm. It was no wonder her fans fell in love so quickly. She had followers of all ages, from toddlers to senior citizens. Everyone was naturally drawn to Hannah Banks.

"Have you ever thought about doing a duet with Eleanor?" Cash asked.

Will perked up. Why hadn't that idea hit him yet? Oh, right. He was too busy telling his body to calm the hell down to think too far ahead. But a duet with her grandmother would be record-breaking, no doubt.

"Actually, we sing together all the time," Hannah admitted. "But only on her back porch on Sunday afternoons. Hallie comes, too. We all sing Grandma's old songs or hymns. It's something we've done since I was a little girl."

Remaking Eleanor's old songs with her megastar granddaughter was certainly something Will would bring up again later. The sales from a project like that would be astronomical.

"Tradition is important," Will commented. "I've never heard your sister sing."

Hannah laughed. "She would never let you. She's good, though. But she isn't one to step into the light. I've tried to get her to come on stage with me or even do background vocals. She refuses."

"Maybe we can convince her," Cash said, and winked. "Can you imagine the fans if you, your sister and your grandmother all took the stage?"

That would be perfect for an awards ceremony. But Will wasn't ready to make everything happen all at once. He had to pace himself and get a feel for how he and Hannah could work together first.

Not getting too ambitious too fast was one of the ways he controlled the situation, and maybe a small part of him still stung from not getting things right years ago, when he was fired from his first position.

Hannah beamed. "That would be amazing, but don't get too attached to that idea."

"Have you been working on practicing the lyrics?" Will asked, trying to circle back to the reason they were all here. Watching Cash and Hannah smile like teenagers at each other was grating on Will's very last nerve.

Her smile faltered and she let out a sigh. "I have been," she admitted. "But there's something that's not quite right with the chorus."

"Let's hear it," Cash said. "I'm the only one who

has sung it so far, so maybe once I hear how you put your melody in, we can think of what needs to be adjusted so we flow together."

"I'm sure it's fine," Will added. "Did you sing with your guitar?"

Hannah nodded and crossed the room to grab her guitar off the stand. She eased one hip onto the stool beneath a mic suspended from the ceiling. As her hair curtained around her face, Will stood mesmerized as she struck that first chord. She lifted her head slightly as her eyes closed and she instantly transformed before him.

Hannah Banks became the music she sang, and as crazy as that sounded, it was true. She wasn't flirty or giddy or smiling—she was feeling every note and every word as she became the song.

She hesitated at the chorus and stopped, looking down to her guitar to find the right chord. Will had heard this song before from Cash, but hearing Hannah sing it was like listening to an entirely different ballad.

Was it any wonder the world loved her so much? She had a sweet Southern twang like Eleanor, but a softness that was all Hannah. Combined with her beauty and her girl-next-door personality, she was the perfect example of a country music sensation.

"Keep going," Will told her. "Don't stop."

Her eyes came up to meet his. "It's not right."

"It's perfect."

He felt it in his soul and that wasn't something

he could say with every artist he worked with. Hannah's music was magical.

"I agree," Cash replied. "You're questioning yourself, but that actually came out better than I'd ever thought or hoped."

Hannah pursed her lips and stared back down at her guitar. When she started the song again, she didn't stop, but she did change up the chorus from how Cash had written it…and the damn thing sounded even better than perfect.

"She's mesmerizing to watch in person," Cash murmured to Will.

Oh, she was mesmerizing all right. Her look, her sound—everything about her could pull in any audience. It was pulling him in, too.

How she managed to do that was astounding.

Just as she finished the last note, Will's phone echoed in the room. Hannah jerked her attention toward him as he pulled the cell from his pocket.

"Sorry about that," he told her. "Just my emails going off. That was…better than I expected."

Her bright smile spread across her face as she tipped her head. He found that familiar gesture both adorable and arousing. How could she be adorable when she sat there in a flaming red jumpsuit that hugged her every curve, with lips that matched, and blond hair teased out all around her? The woman was a vixen and she knew it.

She likely knew that she was getting to him, too. Was she toying with him on purpose?

At least she wasn't pretending to be Hallie anymore, but if he had the choice, he'd almost prefer that she tone it down. He'd take her twin games over this siren for the sake of his sanity.

"What did you think, Cash?"

Shaking his head, Cash chuckled. "I didn't know my song could sound that good."

"I didn't mean to change that last bit on you, but it just came to me as I was singing."

"No, the mix-up of the chords was actually spot on."

She slid off the stool and put her guitar back on the stand, then turned to face them once again.

"Usually when something doesn't feel or sound right to the artist, that's how it will come across to the audience," she explained. "My grandmother drilled that into me at an early age. You want your listeners to feel just as much as you do and you want them to get lost in the story you're telling through your music."

Oh, Will had been lost, all right. Lost in fantasies that he had no place venturing into.

"The way you just did that song, that's how it needs to be on the track and on the tour," Will told her. "We will release that as your first single."

Her smile faltered and she glanced from Will to Cash. "I'm not sure that's the song I want to release first."

Pulling in a deep breath, Will swiped a hand over his jaw. "We put that in your contract."

Hannah nodded. "We did, but I was hoping we could discuss it. There's another song I want to release first."

"Whose song is it?" he asked.

She hesitated for a moment, then replied, "Nobody you know. I heard it and fell in love with it."

"You know that going on tour with Cash is a big deal, so it makes sense for his song to be your first release." Will had made that perfectly clear on the day she'd signed the contract. "Your stage list is up for negotiation, but not that first single."

Hannah's lips thinned and Cash started to speak. Will held up his hand, holding off his little brother.

"None of this is news to you," Will reminded her. "Are we going to have a problem?"

Her eyes glazed over and that sweet, sultry singer was gone. Now she looked like she wanted to wring his neck.

Damn, that was sexy.

Fiery passion simmered below that sweet surface. The woman could switch her emotions so damn fast, he reeled from it.

He couldn't help but wonder how passionate she would be in bed.

Again, he scolded himself for the thought. He'd scolded himself many times for allowing those thoughts to creep into his mind, but everything she did seemed to get under his skin. She affected him in ways no other woman ever had.

He wasn't certain what to do about it.

"How about I play the song first and then you can think about it?" she finally offered.

"I don't mind," Cash muttered.

Will turned to his brother. "It's not your decision to make. The whole reason you sold that song to her was for her to release it as her first single with Elite and that's what we're going to do."

Hannah took a step forward, then another, until she stood within an inch of him. She stared up at him with those doe eyes and bright red lips. He fisted his hands at his sides to keep from reaching for her. But he couldn't stop wondering how she'd look if he kissed the hell out of her and messed up that lipstick. Suddenly, that's all he wanted to do.

Good thing his brother was in the room. Was Will going to need a chaperone each time he was with Hannah?

"You're the boss," she stated with a tone that sounded almost husky, a little threatening and a whole lot sexy.

Oh, he'd give just about anything to be the boss in more intimate ways. Hannah likely wasn't one to give up control in the bedroom, either, which for some reason only stirred him up more.

Will smiled. "Remember that."

Her eyes flared and for a split second her gaze darted to his mouth before sliding back up to meet his eyes. The woman would make a saint have erotic thoughts and he'd never been known as a saint.

Damn it. He was in for a long, painful journey

with her—and that had nothing to do with them butting heads over music.

Cash cleared his throat and pulled Will's attention from the siren in front of him posing as a sweet li'l country girl.

When Will glanced to his brother, Cash was wearing a knowing smirk. No doubt Cash would give Will hell later. He could handle his brother. What Will couldn't handle was these crazy, mixed-up feelings that seemed to come out of nowhere.

"Let's get to work," Will stated, taking a step back. "I want to hear you do that song from start to finish. Then I want to see what it sounds like with Cash doing background vocals on the chorus."

Hannah sneered. "Whatever you say."

Oh, she was going to be a handful.

Will didn't know if he should be eager for the challenge or wary of how aroused he seemed to get when she was angry with him. Either way, Hannah Banks was going to be one unforgettable experience.

Five

"That was amazing," Hannah told Cash as she led him to the door. "See you on Thursday."

Cash leaned in and kissed her cheek. "See you then."

She closed the door behind him. The crowd would go wild over that hunk of country charm. Cash was the entire package—sweet and sexy, broad and built. He had manners and a smile that would make any woman melt.

Hannah turned her attention toward the staircase. The man who got to her even more was up there waiting in the studio because he wanted a private meeting.

Was he going to reprimand her for stating her opinion? Was he upset that she'd contradicted what had been put in the contract?

Whatever it was, he had been clear he would see Cash later, but now he needed to talk to her alone.

A shiver of excitement ran through her as she headed back up to the studio. She shouldn't find his arrogance and dominance so attractive. She should hold her ground and tell him exactly what she wanted. Wasn't finding her own voice and controlling her own career two of the main reasons she'd left Cheating Hearts Records? Mags had governed every aspect of Hannah's career. So much so that Hannah had kept losing more and more of herself as the years passed by.

She was done being told what to do.

Pulling in a deep breath, Hannah stepped back into the studio. Will turned from the system board to face her before he shoved a hand in the pocket of his jeans and met her gaze.

"You guys sound good together."

Hannah rested her hip on the desk near him and laughed. "Good? I sound good in the shower, Will. Cash and I sound like your record label is about to soar into new territory and make you millions."

His gaze seemed to darken as his lids lowered in that sexy manner that made the corners of his eyes wrinkle.

"Do you always sing in the shower?" he asked.

Had his voice just taken on a huskier tone? Why had she tossed out that reference to singing in the shower? There was no denying what was rolling through his head right now, and it had nothing to do with music and everything to do with her being wet and sudsy.

"I sing all the time," she replied. "It's not just a career for me. I love what I do and it shows because I'm good at it."

Will smirked as he took a step closer. "Are you always this sure of yourself?"

"I'm sure of my talent," she replied. "I'm not trying to be arrogant, but I believe my sales will back up my claims."

"Confidence is a big part of this industry," he agreed. "I take back my statement. You and Cash were amazing together."

Hannah smiled. "That's better. I like your brother. Are your other two brothers just as charming?"

Will's eyes narrowed. "Charming? I wouldn't call Gavin and Luke charming."

Intrigued to know more about him and his family, Hannah tipped her head. "Then what would you call them?"

"Career-oriented, sometimes arrogant, sometimes a pain in my ass, but they always have my back."

"They're pretty easy on the eyes, as well," she added. "Yet none of you have girlfriends."

The muscle in Will's jaw ticked. "How do you know that?"

Hannah laughed and rolled her eyes. "Oh, please. This is Beaumont Bay. Nashville has nothing on us. The only thing hotter than the country music is the gossip mill."

"Maybe they're discreet." He crossed his arms over his chest and shifted his stance, clearly getting uncomfortable. "Why the sudden personal interest in my brothers?"

Hannah shrugged. "You know all about my family. Maybe I wanted to know more about yours."

"Your family has been in the spotlight since before you were born."

"Fair enough," she agreed. "All the more reason for me to know about yours. After all, Cash is in the spotlight now. I want to learn more about Luke and Gavin, but let's start with you."

The way he stared at her, like he could read her every thought, had Hannah backing up until she bumped into the stool. She eased onto it and continued to wait for Will to say something.

The silence surrounding them was too much. Her heart beat faster than it should have and her stomach twisted into knots. His intense stare made her thoughts simply vanish. She found herself focusing on his face—those striking eyes that were boring into her, that square jawline, the stubble that he hadn't shaved for probably the past three days.

And then there were his lips. Those lips that had her staring far too long and fantasizing far too much. A man like Will, who was so dominant in everything he did, would surely kiss a woman with just as much power and passion.

And what about in the bedroom? Oh, she knew

without a doubt that the man would be dominant and demanding.

Hannah shivered and closed her eyes, trying to compose herself.

"What do you want to know about me?"

Hannah opened her eyes, startled that Will had moved closer and was now standing within touching distance…and she so wanted to touch.

So she did.

Hannah reached up, sliding her fingertip between his eyebrows.

"I want to know why those worry lines never seem to go away."

Will gripped her wrist and slowly eased her hand away, but he didn't release her. Instead, he took a step closer, so close she had to spread her legs to give him standing room.

"Concerned for me?" he murmured.

Hannah swallowed. "More concerned for my career," she amended. "I can't have you stressed when you're around me."

Her eyes dropped to his lips, then back up. She didn't mean to. She just couldn't stop staring at that mouth.

"And you think looking at me like you want to kiss me is keeping me calm?"

Hannah's breath caught in her throat.

She hadn't anticipated him being so bold, but she shouldn't have been surprised. A man in Will's position wouldn't back down from a challenge or avoid confrontation. And why should he? His confidence was just another turn-on.

But this was dangerous territory, so she reined her emotions back in.

"Your ego is clouding your judgment," she replied. "I don't want to kiss you."

He quirked an eyebrow as his mouth curved into a smile. "No?"

Hannah tipped her chin and opened her mouth—

Then he covered her lips with his, cutting off anything she'd been about to say.

Hannah had to brace her hands on Will's shoulders to keep from falling backward off the stool. He didn't touch her anywhere but her mouth as he coaxed her lips wider and claimed her with only a kiss.

Her entire body tightened as she curled her fingers into him. The warmth from his touch did something to her she couldn't even describe. Her head spun. She didn't know the last time anyone had caught her off guard the way this man just had.

Will pulled back just as quickly as he'd come in. Hannah blinked, trying to catch her breath and figure out what the hell just happened. Other than the fact that she'd just kissed her new record producer—and only wanted more—she had no idea what to do next.

Was stripping and begging too forward?

Clearly battling his own inner turmoil, Will paced the studio, cursing beneath his breath. With his back to her, he placed his hands on his hips and dropped his head between his shoulders.

Hannah stared across the space, barely resisting the urge to touch her fingertips to her still tingling lips. The kiss had lasted only a moment, but the effect of his touch was far more potent than she could have imagined.

Will raked a hand over the back of his head and turned around. His eyes focused on her and seemed darker, as if some inner storm brewed within him.

"That can't happen again," he growled.

"Um...okay." Confused, Hannah came to her feet, but remained near the stool. "You kissed me, so are you reminding yourself?"

Something dark flashed through his eyes and she couldn't help but be drawn to that simple reaction that showed so much frustration.

Who the hell was he upset with? She certainly hadn't initiated anything. Well, in her mind she had already undressed him and explored every inch of that broad, built body, finding out firsthand if he was as rock-hard as he appeared.

But she'd refrained from tearing off his clothes in actuality...barely.

That wouldn't exactly be the best way to start a working relationship.

Both of their phones chimed at the same time.

They continued to stare at each other and Hannah had to break eye contact. She couldn't keep looking at him, not now that she'd tasted him and knew how easily his facade could disappear.

Which made her wonder how long he'd wanted to kiss her and when he would kiss her again. Because there would most certainly be a next time…despite that little speech he'd just given to himself.

Hannah went to the counter and pulled up her phone, groaning when she saw the text from Mags.

"She's insufferable," Hannah mumbled.

"I have one from her, too."

Hannah glanced over her shoulder to see Will opening his message. What was Mags up to now? Group texting like a jealous teen who wanted to keep everyone together?

When Hannah opened the text, she saw an image and realized it was an invitation. Apparently, Margaret Dumond wanted to throw an elaborate fundraiser to help rebuild the parts of town hurt by the recent storm. Mags would do anything for the spotlight, even pose as a caring citizen.

Mags did all she could to stay in the know when it came to this lakeside community. The woman knew everything from when someone found out they were pregnant to when someone was cheating. There wasn't a whisper of gossip that didn't pass through her lips or ears.

The FBI had nothing on Mags.

The invitation indicated there would be various auctions with donations taken at the door and Mags would have all the necessary press there for publicity, which was how she would sucker everyone who was anyone into coming.

Mags wasn't an evil woman, though she was known to be ruthless and conniving to get what she wanted. But the majority of the time she was just bossy, nosy and believed herself to be on a higher pedestal than anyone else. That wasn't the type of woman Hannah wanted to be in charge of her career, but the party would help raise funds for the town and there would be speculation if all of Beaumont Bay's elite crowd wasn't in attendance.

Even with her manipulative ways, Hannah couldn't completely despise Mags. The woman had given Hannah her first record deal and several years in a dream profession. But their outlooks were different at this point and that's why Hannah had to step away and protect herself.

"Looks like we're going to a party," Will stated as he slid his cell back into his pocket.

"Oh, not just any party," Hannah corrected. "A black-and-white charity ball."

Will snorted. "It can't just be a regular fundraiser with that woman. You know, like an afternoon barbecue or a festival around the lake to involve kids and families. This is Beaumont Bay, first of all. Second of all, Mags always goes over the top. Stars, power brokers, moguls—she invites all the names. She has to provide top entertainment when they get there."

The woman thrived on being extra. Good, bad,

she didn't care. She could spin anything to shine light on herself.

"Do you want to talk about it?" he asked.

Hannah set down her phone and smiled. "Sure. I'm thinking of wearing white because probably most people will wear black—"

"You know what I mean."

Oh, she knew what he meant, but no, she didn't want to talk about *the kiss*. She wouldn't mind having a do-over, though. Maybe she'd just imagined how amazing and toe-curling he had been. Maybe that tingling stemmed from something else and not Will's lips on hers for the briefest of moments.

He hadn't touched her anywhere else. That fact kept shoving to the forefront of her mind, as if to ask her why *just a kiss* should have given her such a strong reaction. And she hadn't even attempted to stop him…not that she'd wanted to.

Mercy, she'd wanted him to.

All those wants and needs were becoming a wedge she didn't need landing between them. She had to form a bond with her producer so they could crank out the best music of her career and keep making those chart toppers.

Instead, she was having naive fantasies and couldn't even concentrate on work unless Cash was in the room as a buffer.

"I don't think talking about the kiss is necessary," she replied. "It was good, but we're done."

His eyebrows drew in. "Good? You call that kiss just good?"

Oh, she'd offended him now. That was an interesting kernel of information to save for later.

"Yeah, good," she repeated. "You know…like my singing."

Will narrowed his eyes before taking a step forward, then another, until he came to stand within an inch of her.

Hannah's heart started beating faster and anticipation had her licking her lips.

He leaned down, so close that Hannah arched just a little, waiting on him to close that small gap between them. His warm breath washed over her and she could practically taste him.

"That kiss was just as epic and damn amazing as your singing," he murmured.

And then he walked away.

Out of the studio, out of her house. She heard the door close below and realized she'd been holding her breath.

Damn that man for making her get all worked up. Common sense told her this was all a bad idea, that kissing her producer would only lead to trouble down the road.

But that didn't stop her from wanting more.

Hannah went to her notebook and jotted down more lyrics. And why wouldn't she? She now found herself smack-dab in the middle of living her own damn country song.

Six

"The man is insufferable," Hannah complained.

Hallie continued searching through the rack of clothes without missing a beat.

"You've said that three times since we left your house. Care to tell me what the problem is?"

Hannah wasn't in the mood to shop. When Hallie had called earlier and wanted to pop over to the Vintage Closet, Hannah agreed. The newest boutique in the Bay was all the rage...and was owned by a distant cousin of Dolly herself. Everyone in this area and in Nashville usually knew each other or could relate to each other somehow through the country music industry. Everything tied back to music, no matter the profession.

This girls' day out was good. Hannah had needed

to hit up some new shops and grab lunch at Cowbells and Shotgun Shells. Despite the name, the place was an upscale café with the absolute best wraps and smoothies.

Hannah had needed to get out of the house. She'd needed to get away from that lyric notebook and all of her intimate thoughts.

Since Will left yesterday, Hannah had written two songs, both about wanting a man she couldn't have. Could she be any more clichéd?

Wanting Will wasn't necessarily the problem. The problem stemmed from the fact they were both industry professionals who were just starting to work together and neither needed the black cloud of suspicion that would roll over their heads if they got involved romantically.

Every move Hannah made was splashed across social media before she could take her next breath. The public was always interested in celebrities' lives—in her case, from the lavish parties she attended to the strolls she made around the lake to clear her head. She had to be careful about being seen with any man because speculations would rise and rumors would spread.

When Jake Carver, celebrity trainer, had moved to Beaumont Bay, she'd instantly hired him. That started tongues wagging, but he was just a good friend. He worked with everyone in the Bay to keep them in shape. The man was sexy as hell, but not her type.

Will wasn't her type, either. He couldn't be.

Hannah would much rather people talk about her career and her songs as opposed to her personal life, but that wasn't how her world worked, not to mention living in this close-knit lakeside community. Here, certain members just loved to circulate any excitement they could find.

"You're not talking."

Hannah blinked and noted her sister was holding a yellow sundress in one hand and a plain green jumpsuit in the other, but was staring across the rack at Hannah.

"I'm thinking," Hannah grumbled.

She also blamed Will for putting her in this bad mood. She couldn't even get her thoughts together to form a coherent sentence and if she didn't get her act together, Hallie was going to pick up on her concerns.

Hannah didn't like keeping secrets from her sister. In fact, she never did. But right now, she wasn't ready to disclose what had happened or how it was making her feel.

"I'm not typically a grouchy person," Hannah added.

Hallie laughed. "Are you asking me or telling me?"

Hannah shrugged. "I don't even know anymore. You see? He's even got my thoughts all crazy."

"Oh, no."

Hannah jerked slightly. "'Oh, no,' what?"

"You like him," Hallie accused, then lowered her voice. "You like *you-know-who*."

Hannah glanced around and only saw two sales ladies who were assisting other customers.

She leaned in, bracing her hand on the rack. "I do not," she said through gritted teeth. "Didn't you hear a word I said? He's irritating and makes me crazy."

"Yeah, just like I said. You like him."

Hannah rolled her eyes. "I do not. I mean, I want him to help me launch this next phase of my career, but other than that, I don't want him in my personal life."

"So how did he land there?" Hallie asked with a smile. "You put him smack-dab in the middle of your personal life, right?"

Hannah sighed. "I didn't mean to, damn it. I certainly didn't mean for him to kiss me."

"What?"

Hallie came around the rack and stood right next to Hannah.

"What did you just say?" Hallie asked again.

Hannah realized what had just slipped out and she shook her head. So much for keeping a secret.

"Forget it. I didn't say anything."

"Oh, you certainly did. Now tell me everything." Hallie glanced around as a new customer came into the store. "Okay, maybe wait until we get back in the car for privacy, but you will tell me every single detail."

Suddenly Hannah wasn't in a hurry to leave and

shopping wasn't such a bad idea. Maybe if she stuck around here for a while Hallie would forget she'd said anything.

Wishful thinking.

Hannah reached for something on the rack without paying any attention to size or style. She needed an escape, so the dressing room would have to suffice. Besides, she wanted to find some new things for a photo shoot coming up and maybe something new for Mags's charity event. Plus, there was the album cover she would be shooting soon. Not as if she didn't have enough clothes sent to her from designers, but right now, she planned on spending a good amount of time in the dressing room until she figured out what to tell Hallie.

"I'm going to try on some things," she announced.

Hallie narrowed her eyes. "Oh, now you're interested in looking?"

"I need a few new things."

Hallie laughed. "Oh, please. You know you just got a huge shipment from New York from your favorite designer."

It was true. Designers sent her their upcoming seasonal styles all the time. Anytime a celebrity of her caliber wore a brand in public, that was free publicity. Hannah usually kept her favorite pieces and donated the rest to charity fundraisers.

Still, spending some non-work time with her sister was always necessary. Nobody got Hannah the way

Hallie did. No one understood Hannah's quirks and who she really was behind the bling and makeup.

Which was why Hannah needed to sort out her thoughts before she figured out what to tell her sister. Maybe she needed twin advice. Maybe Hallie would offer some miracle plan to keep Will from invading her every thought.

"Just tell me this," Hallie went on, keeping her voice low. "Was he a good kisser?"

Hannah couldn't help but smile, but quickly bit her lip to try to hide it. She could practically still feel his strength, the warmth of his touch.

"Oh, girl," Hallie laughed. "You are in trouble."

Yeah, that's precisely what Hannah was afraid of. Trouble. Too bad that country song had already been written.

Will walked through the carnage of what used to be his recording studio. The construction crew was hard at work, but this place was going to take a while to recover.

Thankfully, his home had been spared any damage. Other homes around the lake weren't so lucky. Some of the million-dollar mansions were having extensive work done and construction crews from all over the region were all hard at work trying to fit in everyone and their high demands. Many homeowners were also taking this opportunity to do add-ons and go even bigger than before.

That was such a Beaumont Bay thing. Bigger was

always better and so was more bling. They might love their well-worn cowboy boots, but they also loved the glitz and glam of their high-profile lifestyles.

"Mr. Sutherland."

Will turned toward the forewoman. "Morning, Carrie."

She greeted him with a smile as she approached. "It's a mess, but don't worry, we're still on track to be finished by the projected date."

They were nearing the end. That's all he needed to see the light at the end of this dark tunnel. He wasn't sure how she'd pull it off, but he trusted her. He couldn't wait to get back in here and have everything all shiny and new. He planned on throwing an open house, inviting all of his artists and other top-level industry professionals.

That was another commonality here in the Bay. Someone was always hosting a party for one reason or another. Residents and high rollers from the outside were always ready to mingle and chat or show off their latest accomplishment.

"I'll trust you on this one," he laughed as he stepped around a pile of stacked tiles. "Rehabs certainly aren't in my wheelhouse."

"You're in luck, because this is what I love doing."

He'd heard Carrie's construction company was the absolute best. The new studio would be even bigger and better than the last and the lobby area was get-

ting a complete overhaul, as well. Pretty much the only thing staying the same was his office.

"I've ordered all of the new equipment," he told her. "I had it delivered to my house, so just let me know when to get it transferred over here."

Carrie nodded. "Anytime works. I can send my crew over to pick it all up. But I'm glad you stopped by. I wanted to discuss a few of the electrical outlets and lighting positions with you that I think might actually work better than what we originally drew up."

Will followed her around the area, going over the permanent placement of various pieces of equipment. His cell vibrated in his pocket several [illegible] ignored it. This studio was top priority right now and he would answer texts or [illegible] calls later.

Likely it was just Hannah…the woman who hadn't left his mind since he'd left her house. And he'd left in such a damn hurry because he was afraid if he'd stayed any longer, he would have done a hell of a lot more than just kiss her.

That had been a line he never should have crossed.

He tried to focus on Carrie and what she was telling him. Never in his life had anything distracted him from his work. Hannah Banks was not the first beautiful artist he'd had on his label, but she was the only one who had ever gotten under his skin, in his head, and twisted all of his thoughts into a jumble of inappropriateness.

Once he was done with Carrie, Will left the studio, feeling much better about the renovations. The

next few weeks might be a pain in the ass, but in the long run, his professional life would be better because of all the new changes.

His artists were all understanding people and other than Hannah, he didn't have anyone recording in the next couple weeks. That didn't mean he wasn't itching to get back to his normal routine.

As he drove toward his house, his cell rang. Will tapped the screen on his dash and answered the speaker.

“This is Will.”

“[illegible] professional.”

Hannah's sultry voice filled his car and sent shivers through him. He wasn't even face-to-face with the woman and she still had the ability to tap-dance on every sexual nerve he had. How the hell did he intend to keep this relationship professional and his hands off of her?

There would be no greater test of his willpower than Hannah Banks.

“Good morning, Hannah. What can I do for you?”

“I never took you for the type to ask loaded questions,” she mocked.

Will took a turn toward the lake. He waved to one of his neighbors who was pulling out of the gated community and nodded to the gate guard. Will passed the high-end shops that were always hopping with locals wanting the latest fashions. He forced himself to take a couple of deep breaths before replying.

"Hannah, even though I'm a busy man, I'll always have time for my artists, but did you call to play games?"

Her sultry laughter flooded his car and his jeans were getting much too tight for comfort. He'd thought meeting in person was bad, but hearing her voice in stereo was just as much torture.

"I do love a good game, but I did call for a purpose. Hallie received an email from *Craze Magazine*. Apparently I've been chosen as one of the top ten most inspiring female celebrities in the country."

Will turned into his drive and eased into his garage. He put the car in Park and slid off his seat belt, relaxing into his seat.

"That's great news," he told her. "And well-deserved."

"Thank you. They want to do some photos at my house next week and I know we're working on an entirely new album and style, so I need to get your input on the look we need to go for."

Will had a look in mind, but nothing that wouldn't get him a lawsuit slapped in his face. Why did he let those damn images and fantasies creep into his mind? None of this was professional or even how he'd ever reacted to any of his artists before.

"Do you have something in mind?"

"I'm so glad you asked," she replied.

He could practically see her beaming, signature smile.

"With Cheating Hearts I was always known for

rhinestones and the bling," she went on. "I still need to be glam and over-the-top because that's who I am, but maybe in a more sophisticated way. Something that shows I've grown up, but that I'm still country, down-to-earth and relatable to my fans."

And that was one of the many reasons he wanted Hannah Banks on his team. The woman could sing like a thousand angels and she was more beautiful than any woman he knew, but she had a smart business head on those slender shoulders. She actually cared about every aspect of her career and that was something he most definitely appreciated.

He thought her idea sounded perfect and her fans would love this new angle Hannah was taking. He knew she wanted to transition from teen/early twenties icon into the mature woman she had become while in the spotlight.

"I'm on board with all of that," he told her. "How about I come over later and we handle the details?"

"Hallie is here now and we're discussing some ideas. I'm supposed to meet some friends for a brunch tomorrow so let's do this evening. I want to get the setting and theme perfect so I have time to decide what to wear."

"I have a few things to do, but I'll try to get by later."

"No worries."

Will hung up and mentally rearranged his evening plans. He also attempted to prepare himself for another trip to Hannah's house and another evening alone with the woman he couldn't get out of his every fantasy.

At least he'd be going in knowing exactly the impact she had on him. They would remain professional. He had an image to protect, a label, and other artists to worry about, and tarnishing any reputation—hers or his—at this point would be career suicide.

Hannah Banks would just have to remain a fantasy because nothing good would come from a fling…no matter how bad he wanted her.

"I don't like it."

Hannah stared at Hallie in the pale pink strapless maxi dress. The whole identical-twin thing often came in handy. Hannah would have Hallie try things on so Hannah could get a good idea of exactly how things would look to others for various occasions.

Now they were in Hannah's bedroom with clothes strewn over the bed, cluttering the chaise, hanging off all the doorknobs. Nothing seemed to be working for the vision Hannah wanted. But the main problem was she didn't even know what she wanted. She was hoping some inspiration would hit her as she watched Hallie try on different outfits.

"What about that white one-shoulder jumpsuit?" Hallie suggested. "Put that with some gold accessories and a simple manicure and you have both rich and classy."

Hannah did love that jumpsuit that had come in

from one of her favorite designers. She'd been waiting for the perfect opportunity to wear it. Dominic would certainly love it if she sported that for the magazine spread.

"Try that on, then," Hannah suggested. "I'm going to put on that strapless black dress. You know the one that is a little Audrey Hepburn, a little Marilyn Monroe?"

Hallie pursed her lips. "I'm not sure that's the image you want to go for, sis."

At this point, Hannah didn't know what she wanted. The original idea she had in her head seemed to be falling apart. She'd been in countless magazines over the years, she'd been splashed all over the internet in her best and worst outfits, but knowing she could guide this new look was so exciting. This spread would be celebrating women and Hannah wanted to get the vibe just right.

Besides, this photo shoot would be her first chance to show off a new look related to the upcoming album launch. Everything had to be just right from the start. She didn't want to let her fans down and she didn't want to let Will down. That had nothing to do with her personal feelings and everything to do with her professional strategy.

Damn it. As much as she was irritated at herself for getting caught up in her wayward thoughts about Will, she couldn't help but wonder if there was something there. Was he attracted to her more than he let on? Had that kiss affected him like it had affected her? Did he even want to explore this…whatever this was?

She didn't miss the way he stared at her…or the way he got irritated with her. Maybe that's how he coped with attraction? Weird, but men were an odd species.

Despite all of these questions and her own selfish needs, she knew deep down that a fling or even a relationship—if they did give in to one—would be leaked to the public somehow. Nothing stayed private in Beaumont Bay and if word crept out that she was sleeping with her producer, Hannah couldn't even imagine the damning headlines.

That was the last thing she needed when she was trying to reinvent herself and prove she controlled her own career.

Her cell rang and she glanced around until she spotted the device peeking beneath a dress on her bed. She smiled at the name on the screen, then answered.

"Gram, how are you?"

"Well, I need a small favor if you're not too busy."

Eleanor Banks rarely asked anyone for anything, but when she did, people never told her no. Not the music industry, not her husband, not her granddaughters.

Hannah met Hallie's eyes and shrugged. "Sure, what do you need? Hallie is here with me."

"Well, I just got to dinner with some friends and received a notification that a package I've been waiting for is going to be delivered before six. Is there any way you could go to the house, sign for it, and then put it inside? I'm so sorry, honey. I thought it was due tomorrow."

"No need to apologize," Hannah replied. "What am I signing for?"

Eleanor laughed. "You always were the nosy one. It's a one-of-a-kind painting I had shipped from Milan and I wanted to hang it on the wall over the staircase to replace that ghastly one that was given to me a few years ago. I think I've let it run its course, don't you?"

Hannah laughed. "I'll get it taken care of. Enjoy your dinner."

Hannah disconnected the call and blew out a sigh. "I'm going to Gram's really quick to wait and sign for a package."

"Want me to go instead?" Hallie asked.

"Nah. Just stay here and keep working through this mess if you don't mind. Maybe you can narrow down the choices to five instead of all fifty we seem to have out."

Hallie nodded. "I don't mind a bit. I'm really excited for you."

Hannah smiled. "I know you are. You're really the best sister and friend I could've ever asked for."

"You're right, I am," Hallie laughed. "Go on, I'll figure out the perfect outfit while you're gone."

"I'll be right back."

Hannah hoped the delivery didn't take too long.

She really wanted to get back and figure out the photo shoot. Then she wanted to get Will's opinion after she decided. She couldn't help but wonder what Will thought she looked best in. What would he choose for this new angle in her sound and look? Something sexy and sultry with a new country feel or something classic and timeless like old school country?

Everything she did, every thought she had, circled back to Will. When she had been with Cheating Hearts, Hannah certainly hadn't thought of Mags all the time.

Working with Will was going to be an entirely different ball game and Hannah wasn't so sure she was ready for this crazy ride she'd set into motion.

When she'd decided to leave Cheating Hearts, she'd immediately thought of Elite. Will Sutherland was the top man in the industry. He and Elite had worked with some legends and she knew he could take her brand in a new direction.

The Sutherland brothers all worked in the industry in one manner or another and she wanted to be a part of that. She wanted her label to feel like a family and not like a monarchy.

Hannah wasn't quite sure how things would play out with Will on a personal level. One thing was certain, though—she would most definitely not be bored.

From the very beginning she worried about her attraction to Will. Now she had all of this heat between them to contend with and it was already hotter than anything she'd ever envisioned.

Seven

Will punched in the code to Hannah's front gate and let himself in. She'd told him she'd be home trying on things and figuring out the best option for the photo shoot. She'd mentioned wanting his opinion and he'd tried ignoring that pull. He'd even had a mental pep talk with himself about just staying home and letting her sort it out.

Yet here he was, pulling up to her front entrance like some damn high-school kid with a crush on the popular girl.

He was the CEO of a multimillion-dollar record label. What the hell was he doing letting Hannah get to him this way? It wasn't as if he'd never worked with a powerful, beautiful, strong-willed woman before.

Maybe he liked that challenge. Maybe he found

Hannah more intriguing than he cared to admit. Maybe he liked her a little more than in just a professional capacity. That was fine, right? He should like the people he worked with.

But she was the only colleague he had sexual fantasies about…so whatever he was feeling, it went well beyond the simplicity of the like zone.

Will shoved aside any inappropriate thoughts about his newest artist and headed toward her front door. He rang the bell and took a step back to wait.

Moments later, the door swung wide and Hannah appeared, looking to be out of breath.

Then he caught sight of her outfit. It was body-hugging and long. It draped over her shoulders, leaving them exposed. The sleeves were long, but the damn thing still showed off every single curve.

"Will," she exclaimed, clearly surprised. "What are you doing here?"

He stepped in without waiting on the invite. "Since we talked, I thought I'd help you. Remember? You asked me to?"

"Actually—"

"I don't think that's the dress you should wear for the shoot. Too sexy and that's not the vibe you want to give off for this particular piece."

Hannah's shoulders squared, her lips thinned, and she stared at him. "Is that so? Well, I'll have you know this dress is definitely in the running for my favorite so far. I have tried on the entire closet."

"I haven't seen any and you asked for my help." He glanced toward the staircase. "Lead the way."

Hannah laughed. "If you think I'm just going to lead you to my bedroom, you're out of your mind."

Will rolled his eyes. "I didn't think you would try them on in front of me, but I should at least see what outfits you are thinking about."

Hannah pursed her lips and crossed her arms, as if she was unsure about this whole situation. Something wasn't right, and Will had no idea what game she was playing now.

"I don't think you need to come upstairs," she replied, then motioned toward the front room. "How about you wait in there and I'll bring down some options?"

That was it. That was what was off. This wasn't Hannah at all—it was Hallie.

No way in hell would Hannah give up on an argument so easily. She would order him to do something and argue if he disagreed. Hallie had always been rumored to be the sweet sister and there was the proof right before his eyes.

And now that he knew what was going on, he could see that Hannah and Hallie had even more differences than he'd realized. Hannah's curves were a bit more prominent, something difficult to tell considering Hallie typically didn't wear body-hugging dresses.

So where was Hannah?

He pulled out his cell and started typing.

"What are you doing?" she asked.

Without looking up, he replied, "I don't like these games."

"Games?"

He sent off a text to Hannah and pocketed his cell before turning his attention back to Hallie.

"Where's your sister?" he asked.

Hallie's eyebrows drew in and she jerked slightly. "Uh…she's at our Gram's house. Why?"

"Because this switch she keeps doing with me is getting ridiculous."

Hallie narrowed her stare and crossed her arms. "So you know I'm Hallie?"

"Not at first," he admitted. "But I do now. Does she find this amusing or is this something you both do often?"

Hallie shrugged. "Not so much now that we're adults. It certainly came in handy during school or with Gram when we were younger and one of us was in trouble."

Oh, he had no doubt those two pulled off some schemes during their teens. He and his brothers had been quite a handful as well, and he couldn't imagine what would have happened if two of them had been identical.

"Your sister posed as you last week," Will stated. "Are you aware she does that?"

Hallie laughed and dropped her arms. "No, I wasn't, but I'm not surprised. Sometimes she doesn't want to be recognized, so if she dressed calmer, like I do, then she doesn't get bothered too much."

Will could understand that…to a point. Not so much when she was supposed to be meeting with her new record producer.

His cell vibrated in his pocket, but he ignored it. Let Hannah sweat just a little. He might not want to be part of her little games, but she was the one who'd pulled him into this and made him a player whether he liked it or not.

His frustration level with her was starting to reach an all-time high.

"How about I wait on Hannah here, and you can go," he suggested.

Hallie quirked an eyebrow—that was such a Hannah move. Damn, these two could easily fool someone…but not him. Not now that he knew exactly how Hannah moved, her irritated facial expressions, the curves of her body…and the way his body reacted to her.

"You're dismissing me?" she asked in a tone that suggested he'd just made a serious mistake.

Will shrugged. "I'm not trying to be disrespectful, but I want to have a private conversation with Hannah when she gets home. You might not want to be here."

Hallie's face split into a smile. "Oh, I'd love to be here for that, but I actually am about done upstairs. I will call her later and discuss my thoughts on the magazine shoot. We had almost figured it out before she left."

"And where did you say she went?"

"Gram called and needed her to run over for a bit," Hallie replied as she turned toward the steps. "She should be back anytime. I'm going to go change and get out of here."

Will watched as she disappeared and shook his head. How in the hell had he thought Hallie was Hannah, even for a moment? There was a little lilt in Hallie's voice that Hannah didn't have. Hannah would cock her head to one side when something irritated her, whereas Hallie seemed to throw daggers with an intense glare.

Will turned in the foyer and glanced around as he made his way into the front room. He hadn't been in this room before so he took this opportunity to get to know more about Hannah.

Surprisingly, her decor was rather simple compared to her wardrobe. The white sofas with pale gray pillows and green potted plants of various sizes and styles seemed to be calming and relaxing. He didn't see one piece of evidence showing Hannah the superstar. There were family photos here and there, with a few along the mantel, which drew his attention.

Will crossed the room to examine them further and couldn't help but smile at a young Hannah and Hallie dressed up standing on either side of Eleanor Banks as she held one of her many prestigious awards. The girls appeared to be about five if he had to guess. He didn't know much about children, but they were small with missing front teeth and huge grins.

He moved to the next photo and saw a little older Hannah and Hallie, one of them putting makeup on Eleanor while the other one seemed to be curling her hair.

As he glanced around, Will realized all of the photos were of the twins and their grandmother. There was no doubt family was the foundation of Hannah's life.

Will knew Hannah's parents had left when the twins had been younger. They'd gotten business opportunities and were so busy traveling, the girls went to live with Eleanor to have a stable lifestyle. She didn't mention them much in public and she'd said nothing to him. All he knew was her close relationship with her grandmother.

He recalled that the media loved capturing Eleanor out and about with her granddaughters when they'd be heading to their private school or going to an awards shows.

No doubt that's what had led the girls into this life in the music industry. It was no wonder they shared such a solid, special bond with Eleanor.

Family was another area he and Hannah had in common. His brothers were everything to him. They might butt heads now and then, but overall, they were always a solid unit. He knew at any time Gavin,

Luke, and Cash would always have his back and he would have theirs.

"Will."

He turned to see Hallie in the wide, arched doorway. She'd changed from the body-hugging dress to a pair of jeans and a simple green sweater.

"Just a warning," she went on. "Mags ran Hannah's life for so long that I don't want that to happen to her again."

Interesting. The quiet sister getting bolder and bolder. Maybe she was the backbone of the duo…or maybe the twins were each other's backbone.

"You think I'm going to control her?" he asked.

"I'm not sure yet," Hallie admitted with a shrug. "I know you want to make money and Hannah will definitely do that for you. I just know she has other aspirations, too."

More aspirations than being the biggest star in country music, rivaling her own grandmother? She hadn't shared any of those aspirations with him, other than wanting to cultivate a more mature sound. Was there more? If she had such goals, that should've come up during their contract negotiation process or when she'd first approached him.

"If she wants me to know something, she should tell me."

Hallie pulled in a breath and tipped her chin. "She's more vulnerable than most people think."

Will took a step toward her, keeping his eyes locked on Hallie's. "Everyone has a vulnerable spot."

"Maybe so, but not everyone is thrust into the limelight to have theirs exposed," Hallie retorted. "Hannah isn't as confident as she wants everyone to believe."

Not confident? The woman was *too* confident. She was bold, daring, passionate, and in-your-face. Lack of confidence was definitely not a vibe he'd ever gotten from her.

She sure as hell seemed confident when she tipped up her head and silently begged him to kiss her.

The front door opened and closed and suddenly Hannah filled the doorway next to her sister. Her eyes darted between the two.

"A meeting without me?" she asked with a smile. "Sorry I'm late. Who wants to fill me in?"

Yeah, now side-by-side, Will could definitely see the subtle differences. Aside from what they were both wearing—and Hannah had on one killer dress—they each had their own look.

"I was just leaving," Hallie announced as she turned to face her sister. "The white dress has to be in the top two choices. I put that pink wrap maxi dress out, as well. I think you should consider it. I tried to pick up as best as I could. We did some damage in there."

Hannah smiled. "Won't be the last time, but thanks for picking up. I could've gotten it."

Hallie reached out and hugged her sister before easing back. "No worries. I'll let you two get to your, um, meeting."

Hannah laughed. “We don’t have a scheduled meeting.”

“We do,” Will corrected. “You told me to stop by.”

Hannah jerked her attention toward him and raised her eyebrows. “You didn’t actually confirm.”

He shrugged. “It was implied.”

The silence seemed to crackle between them as Will refused to look away from her. Was she angry he was here? Well, he was angry she kept turning him on. And now, with her dressed in that damn body-hugging number, neither his anger, nor the attraction he felt, were any different.

Hallie finally broke the tension.

“Okay, well, I’ll just let myself out.”

Moments later, she was gone and Will continued to stare at Hannah. She blinked without making a move. She’d been home for two minutes and already he’d irritated her…or maybe she’d irritated him. Hell, at this point he couldn’t tell.

“So what did you and my sister have to talk about?”

Will started to close the distance between them, his eyes never wavering from hers.

“We covered a good bit while you were gone.”

Hannah’s eyes widened, whether in fear or worry or arousal, he had no clue. At this point he didn’t know all of her quirks and habits…but damn if he didn’t want to.

“Is that right?”

Will stopped just before he reached her and nodded. “Vulnerabilities, insecurities. Why she tried to pose as you when I first arrived.”

Hannah hesitated before she smiled and did that signature head tilt that made him want to lean down and nip at the creamy, exposed juncture between her shoulder and neck.

“Hallie is used to playing the part when people assume she’s me,” Hannah stated simply. “We’ve done it for each other for so long, we just go with it. Especially if it’s something to do with the industry. She’ll just tell me what I need to know. Sometimes I swear she knows more than I do about all of this.”

“She’s your manager,” he replied. “Not you. These are the games I was talking about at the coffee shop. Or did you forget?”

“I didn’t forget anything,” she retorted, her voice raising just enough to know he was getting her riled up. “You didn’t tell me when you were coming for certain, so none of this is on Hallie or me. It’s on you.”

Hannah started to turn away, but he reached for her arm.

“Where are you going?”

She sent him a glare over her shoulder. “I’m going back to my room, where I was before my gram called. Coming with me?”

His entire body tightened at that invitation. There was nothing professional about following her upstairs. They could discuss the ideas down here. They should have Hallie here, as well. Together, they could all talk about this photo shoot.

Instead, Hannah was waiting for a reply and he knew his answer would have irreversible consequences.

"Lead the way."

Eight

Well, this was certainly not her smartest move, but here she was in her bedroom with Will Sutherland.

Hallie had always told her that one day Hannah's bold mouth would get her into trouble. Part of her would love to get into trouble with Will, but then there was that damn common sense that always ruined her fun.

Her inner turmoil had been bouncing all around since meeting Will face-to-face the very first time. Why did she have to battle with herself? Why couldn't she make up her mind and stick to it?

Because the devil on her shoulder was all too tempting, but the angel on the other shoulder wouldn't keep quiet.

"What's with the dress you're wearing?" Will asked.

She turned and couldn't help but laugh. He remained in the doorway, as if stepping inside would be literally crossing the point of no return.

"Hallie and I were trying to figure out the perfect outfit for the shoot when Gram called and I just ran over like this."

The way his eyes traveled over her body did nothing to help her remain calm. She wished like hell he'd replace that stare with his hands. What she wouldn't give to have a different relationship with Will. This whole working-together thing was really getting in the way of what she truly wanted.

Hannah certainly wasn't in to flings. She couldn't afford flings in this media-driven world she lived in. Everything she did ended up in the tabloids or online. Having an affair with Will Sutherland would ultimately screw her career all up. With the timing—of her signing with Elite and then getting involved with him—it would most definitely have people talking and wondering if the sexual relationship was what got her to move labels after being with Cheating Hearts for over ten years. They'd all be talking about Will and there'd be no room left for the new image and sound she's sacrificed so much to create.

Not only that, but Mags had also tried to control her every move for years. She was done with being controlled. Yet, if Hannah got intimately involved with Will, that would put him even deeper into her life than anyone had been before. She couldn't afford anyone who wasn't family to be so close to her both personally and professionally.

So, no. Absolutely no sex.

But that didn't stop her from continually wanting the hell out of him.

"Wear something else."

Hannah jerked at his commanding tone. "Excuse me?"

"You're not wearing that for the photo shoot."

Why did his demands get her so irritated? Why did she let him annoy her and turn her on at the same time? How was that even possible?

There was way too much tension rolling through her.

"This is the exact dress I'm wearing," she told him, though she still had no idea what she wanted to have on in the photos.

Now he did take a step into the room. Those blue eyes were locked onto hers as he moved closer.

"No, you're not," he repeated. "It's too sexy and not the look we're going for."

"Sexy?"

A muscle in his jaw clenched as he stopped about a foot away. Hannah waited for him to say something, to do something. She was so charged up, she wished like hell he would make the first move so when they crossed this line, the guilt wouldn't be on her.

When.

Yes, there would be a *when.* This wasn't a question of *if* anymore. Even after the speech she'd literally just given herself, she couldn't ignore the inevitable.

Everything was going to get complicated and there wasn't much Hannah could do to stop it.

Oh, she could say no. She could walk away and have a conversation over the phone after she and her sister zeroed in on the details. This whole photoshoot strategy should be between Hannah and her manager, with maybe a few ideas from her producer.

Right now, though, she was giving Will total control. She'd never done that willingly before, but she found herself wanted to relinquish everything to him.

The irony was not lost on her that she'd hated being controlled by Mags, but she welcomed Will's perspective.

"You know damn well what you look like, Hannah. Don't go fishing for compliments."

"Compliments come to me all the time," she responded. "So does criticism. It's all part of the life I live."

Hannah pulled in a breath, tipped her head, and studied Will's features. That strong jawline, those deep blue eyes framed by dark lashes, and that mouth she was dying to taste…

"I never took you for doling out compliments to your artists," she added. "But you called me sexy, so I'm taking that to mean you find me attractive."

There. She'd placed that kernel of obvious attraction between them—now to see what he did with it.

"Do you want me to find you attractive?"

Oh, he was going to make this difficult. He was going to make her be the one to cross the line. Fine, but when she crossed it, she was pulling him with her.

"I want respect above all else," she told him honestly. "And maybe I do want to know what you think of me on a personal level."

His eyes darkened as he raked his gaze over her. Why wouldn't he just do something already? Did she need to send up a flare to get his attention? Write him an invitation?

"Your fans' compliments aren't enough?" he asked, his voice low and gravelly.

"I'm talking about what *you* think."

He took another step toward her, but Hannah refused to move back. She wanted to feel him, she wanted to challenge him, to make him face this with her and stop the silent battle. If they didn't get this out in the open, the want and curiosity would drive her absolutely mad.

"What I think is that I won't keep doing these games anymore." One more step. "I think I'm done with being pulled in all directions." Another step. "And I'm done with the flirting."

Hannah swallowed and lifted her eyes to meet his. "Flirting?"

"You flirt with everyone," Will stated. "The audience when you're on stage, which I understand is part of the show. But you flirted with Cash the second he got here and you flirt with me every chance you get."

"I'm myself around you," she told him. "And I was myself around Cash. We have a natural chemistry. Isn't that what you want with your artists? Especially two who are going to be touring together?"

Will's lips quirked into a naughty grin and he took a step back…the total opposite of what she wanted him to do.

"Then I guess you aren't flirting with me," he countered. "My mistake."

Somehow she'd screwed this up, but maybe that was for the best. She should cool it, focus on her career and not obsess over getting Will naked and in her bed.

But he was already in her bedroom and her mind was spinning, her heart beating faster than usual. She didn't want to waste this chance.

She hadn't gotten this far in life without taking risks.

Hell, signing with Elite had been risky enough. But now she was seriously considering doing much more with Will than just working together on great music.

Ugh. She needed her guitar and her notebook. She hadn't had this much inspiration in years. Will inspired so many emotions inside her and she needed a place to channel all of that. If it weren't for her music, she didn't know what she'd do with everything she was feeling.

"I need to get to the studio," she told him. "Um… we can do this whole clothing thing later."

"What?" he asked, his eyebrows drawn in.

Wanting, waiting, needing...

The lyrics were practically writing themselves in her head. She had to get this down on paper and work on the chords.

"I'll be in the studio."

Hannah eased around him and left her bedroom. She couldn't get to the studio fast enough. The words just kept flowing. At first she wondered about the tempo, but this had to be catchy, fast, and peppy. She didn't want a slow ballad—she'd written enough of those and kept them hidden.

No, this had to be almost reckless, pretty much like her emotions were right now. This was what had been missing from her secret songs. She'd needed something fun and relatable…and she didn't know a single person who hadn't wanted someone without knowing how to go about it.

For every relationship, there was always that season of need and ache. There was that sweet spot between the initial meet and that first kiss. And it was that first kiss she planned on writing about, planned on singing and performing.

She couldn't wait for it all to come together.

Hannah stepped into the recording part of her studio and sank onto the floor next to her guitar stand. She took the guitar and hit that first chord. Then tried another. She sang a couple lines, trying to find that perfect beat, the perfect sound that would make this special song stand out.

She reached for the notebook and pencil on the small table she kept by her guitar.

After jotting down what she wanted for the chorus, she was playing around with the first verse, but not finding the right opening. Did she want to blast right in or start slow and go in for the big buildup… just like how a first kiss felt?

"That's it," she muttered.

"What inspired you?"

Hannah jerked around to Will standing in the doorway. He was leaning against the frame as if he'd been there a while. She'd been so absorbed in her music, in her thoughts, that she hadn't heard him… and she hadn't thought he'd follow her.

"We were discussing clothes," he went on.

Hannah laughed. "No, we weren't. We hadn't gotten that far yet."

She closed her book and eased it to her side before placing her guitar back in the stand. When she came to her feet, she adjusted the tight dress, but stood in place as Will stepped into the room.

"Why didn't you tell me you wrote music?"

Hannah pursed her lips, unsure how to approach the subject. Writing her own music was her ultimate dream. When she switched labels, she'd planned on having several good pieces to offer and discuss. She wanted to be taken seriously as a songwriter, but she'd never performed her own work before. She'd been afraid to take the next step.

"It's something I was going to discuss with you later," she admitted.

"Why not now?" he asked.

Hannah shrugged. "I'm not ready."

Will stopped and seemed to be studying her… She didn't like this. She didn't like this one-on-one scrutiny. She should be used to being under a microscope, and she was to a point, but now she was alone with Will and discussing her lyrics, her dreams. That was a hell of a lot of exposure and vulnerability.

"I'm here now and I'm ready," he countered. "Let's see what you have."

Hannah's nerves jumbled. She would have to show him at some point, but now that the moment had presented itself, she wasn't so sure about what she had to offer. What if he hated her stuff? What if he told her he didn't believe any of it would work? Giving someone a book of your deepest thoughts and asking them to like it was scary as hell.

She could perform in front of thousands of people on a stage by herself for hours, but she couldn't bring herself to hand over a little notebook to the man who was supposed to help her in every aspect of her career.

When she remained silent, Will moved around her and snatched the notebook off the floor, where she'd left it. She reached for it, but he stepped away.

He held the notebook at his side and eased closer to her.

"We all have to expose ourselves at some point," he told her with that low, calm voice. "Everyone has secret thoughts, secrets wants."

She shivered at his tone, knowing he wouldn't make fun, but that didn't mean he would like what he saw. And the most recent work she was just jotting down was clearly about him.

Hannah closed her eyes. "I'm not ready, Will."

"Are we talking about the music?"

She opened her eyes to see he'd moved in even closer. She could make out the navy flecks in his blue eyes. His warm breath brushed over her face, sending even more tingles through her.

"What else would we be talking about?" she murmured.

He kept his eyes on her as he shifted to put the notebook between them. The second he opened to that first page, Hannah closed her eyes once again... She couldn't look. If she saw any type of negative reaction, she would be crushed. She loved each of the pieces she'd written and she desperately wanted others to love them, as well.

Even Hallie hadn't seen the lyrics.

Hannah bit her bottom lip and glanced down at her feet, then to the glass window into the sound room. She looked anywhere but at Will.

Pages flipped one after another and then stopped. Will's deep intake of breath practically echoed.

"You're very passionate."

Hannah forced herself to focus on him, then she darted her gaze down to the page where he'd stopped.

"I've always been passionate about my work," she told him.

He tapped the page. "This is more than work. This is the passion inside of you for someone that has nothing to do with music. Writing the lyrics is just your therapy."

Busted.

"They are," she agreed.

Will closed the book and dropped it to the floor, then he stepped so close his body brushed hers, and Hannah held her breath.

"Who was this last bit about?" he asked, his eyes darting to her lips. "Who inspired you to want and need so much that you had to rush in here to get your thoughts onto paper?"

Hannah couldn't stand it another second.

"You know damn well who."

And then she kissed him.

Nine

Nothing much surprised Will, but Hannah initiating this kiss sure as hell did. Writing about it, thinking about it, and daydreaming about it were totally different than actually acting on it.

But he was damn glad she had.

Finally.

Since she'd initiated this, Will decided to take charge. There had been too much desire built up inside of him and the anticipation had threatened to overcome him on multiple occasions. The second he'd seen Hannah's lyrics, he'd known exactly how she'd been feeling. She'd managed to capture the thoughts, the feelings, the need, so perfectly.

Will framed her face and tipped her head, needing better access to that mouth he'd been tempted by more and more.

Hannah let out a soft moan and all that did was make Will want even more. He wanted to know exactly how to pleasure her, what her desires were, her fantasies.

He wanted every damn thing.

Will moved his hands to her hips and jerked her against him, bringing their bodies flush together... but it was still not enough. Even with this form-fitting dress she wore, he wanted it gone.

Hannah reached for the hem of his shirt and the second her fingertips slid beneath and found his bare skin, Will took that silent invitation and ran with it.

He eased back and jerked the shirt over his head, then looked to her for any sign of hesitation. But those expressive eyes were full of desire. He wasn't going to worry about the consequences right now. They were both adults and nobody else had to know.

Hannah offered a naughty grin as she reached for the top of her dress and started easing it down her body...and holy hell, she had nothing on beneath.

There she stood, completely bare and even more breathtaking than he'd imagined...and he'd been doing a hell of a lot of imagining.

"You can stand here like this and you were afraid to show me your music?" he asked.

Hannah shrugged. "This is different. Physical is all on the surface. Those lyrics, those were in my heart."

Her heart. That was something he couldn't allow himself to get involved with.

"I'm not looking for anything more than the physical," she went on, obviously picking up on his tension. "I want you, Will. It's simple."

Simple. Nothing about Hannah had been simple since he'd met her. But he did want her, and all the reasons to deny either one of them had long since fled his mind. Prolonging the inevitable would only make them both miserable.

When she reached for the button of his jeans, Will sucked in a deep breath. Her touch seemed so delicate, yet so bold and commanding. She was quite the mix of contradictions and every part of her turned him on. There was no fighting this and he didn't know why he thought he could.

"Will?" she asked. "You with me?"

The way she continued to stare at him, completely exposed, pulled at something deep inside of him. Between the songs and her willingness to cross this line with him, there was some bond they'd already formed that he couldn't delve too far into right now. Letting his mind get involved was a mistake.

Damn the work and damn the consequences.

Will didn't answer with words—instead he quickly undressed and wasted no time in reaching for her. Hannah melted into his embrace as she arched against him. Together they made it to the rug on the floor and Will carefully laid her down beneath him.

Her hair was spread all around her and Will remained up on his knees so he could stare down at her. Right now he wasn't her producer and she wasn't a superstar. They had taken everything down to the basics. He had no idea what would happen after, but he only cared about now.

Hannah reached for him. "Stop thinking," she murmured. "We both need this and anything we do, it stays right here."

"Between us," he agreed.

Hannah nodded and lifted her knees on either side of his hips. "That's all I want."

So why was he still waiting? There was no reason for more talk and there was no reason to worry. It was sex, plain and simple, just like she'd said.

There was that niggle in the back of his mind that kept shooting up warnings saying this was wrong, this shouldn't be happening. But they'd already crossed the line and he planned on seeing them both to the finish line.

"You're thinking again." Hannah tightened her knees against him and arched. "Now, Will."

He gripped her hips and leaned down until his mouth was a breath from hers. He grazed his lips across her jaw, over her chin, and finally landed on hers. She opened for him just as he eased into her and joined their bodies.

A soft moan escaped her once again and it took every bit of willpower for him to remain still. He wanted to capture this moment, to relish in the feel of her sensual body beneath his and all around him.

Hannah threaded her fingers through his hair, holding him in place as she swept her tongue through his mouth. There was nothing sexier than a woman who knew what she wanted and wasn't afraid to go after it.

Perhaps that was why he felt this pull toward Hannah. Of course, she was sexy as hell, but beyond that, her bold personality and determination paralleled his own.

He'd never met a woman like Hannah…and it was becoming quite apparent she was definitely one of a kind.

Will started moving, shifting, and tilting his hips. Immediately, Hannah joined him and they found a perfect rhythm.

Needing more leverage, Will placed one hand beside her head and eased the other behind her knee. He pumped harder, faster, breaking away from her lips so he could watch her. He didn't want to miss a moment of her coming undone.

And from the sounds of her pants and moans and the way she jerked her hips, she wasn't too far off. Which was good, because he didn't know how much longer he would last. They'd been doing silent foreplay and building up to this moment for too damn long. He could work on finesse and longevity later.

Oh, there most definitely would be a later.

"Will," she murmured as she wrapped her free leg across his waist. "Please."

The whispered begging did him in. Will lifted

back up to his knees and gripped her hips so she stayed with him. Then he lifted her backside slightly to give her the best angle and the most pleasing sensations. He wanted to be the one to make her explode, to make her cry out his name.

And she didn't disappoint. Hannah's fingertips dug in to his forearms as she came apart. With her eyes shut, her head tipped back and her body bowed, she was completely vulnerable in a way he'd never thought he'd see. There was something so magnificent about this woman, this moment, but he couldn't focus, not when his own body was following hers.

Will ground his teeth together as he stilled, allowing every glorious sensation to wash over him. Hannah's body was still clenched around him, pulling out all the passion he'd been trying to keep locked away.

Once his body ceased trembling, he glanced down to her and found her smiling up at him. The image of her luscious body, with her hair in disarray, not to mention that he'd kissed off all of her lipstick and had gotten her down to being a little more basic, a little raw, drove him out of his ever loving mind.

Damn it. He shouldn't be attracted to both sides of Hannah, but he was. And he certainly shouldn't be ready to do this all over again, but he couldn't help the need that crept up and overcame him.

Will eased away because the alternative scared the hell out of him. He came to his feet and reached down, offering Hannah his hand.

Once he helped her to her feet, she picked up her

dress and promptly shimmied back into it. Now he'd never look at the damn thing again without remembering this moment. There was no way she could wear that for any photo shoot, or album cover, or anything else where people could see her in it. This dress was meant for his eyes only.

"Now what?" she asked as he started to dress.

Will buttoned his jeans and tugged his T-shirt over his head. "Do you want to talk about it?"

Oh, please say no. There was nothing worse than fast, frantic sex and then rehashing it all in some awkward conversation that only ended in both of them feeling weird.

"Talk about it?" she asked. "Honey, I'll sing about it."

Then she laughed and refluffed her hair to fall around her shoulders. She looked like she'd just come from her lover's bed…and his entire body tightened once again.

How did she do that to him? On one hand, he was glad she'd laughed and made a joke, but on the other hand, he wanted to peel her back out of that dress.

"That would be a first," he told her.

"What? Nobody has made a song about sex with you before?" she asked with that wide grin. "I find that difficult to believe. Maybe we should try it again later in case I forget just how amazing it was."

Again with that bold nature of hers.

"You think it would be smart to do it again?" he asked.

Hannah shrugged. "It wasn't smart to do it the first time, but we did. We both liked it, so why should we stop? We can keep this separate from the working relationship, can't we?"

Hell, he didn't know. He was a guy. He hadn't thought that far ahead. How could this sexual connection not affect their working relationship? Wouldn't people pick up on the chemistry between them? What if he touched her or looked at her the wrong way and someone figured out their secret?

"I can see you need to think this over," she added. "How about we work on the photo-shoot ideas?"

Work. Yes. He needed to circle back to something he could control, because as ready as he thought he was for another sexual encounter with Hannah, tonight hadn't prepared him at all.

And now she wanted more.

What the hell should he do with that information?

"How angry was Will yesterday?" Hallie asked.

Hannah twirled the stem of her empty wineglass and sighed. "Angry? I wouldn't say that."

Turned on, one of the best lovers she'd ever had, a man she couldn't wait to jump again? That pretty much described him, but even with her twin, Hannah wasn't ready to announce what had happened.

"He was a little irked when he thought I was you and that we had played him," Hallie went on.

Hallie and Hannah had gone over to their gram's house for an afternoon lunch and some girl time.

Eleanor had stepped inside to grab the dessert and Hannah had been waiting for her sister to bring up the encounter with Will.

"Since we all have to work together for the good of your career, I really don't want to piss him off," Hallie stated. "But he was kind of cute when he was ticked."

"Oh, he's cute," Hannah agreed.

And sexy and delicious.

"His brothers aren't bad, either," Hallie added. "How can they *not* be attractive with all that power and sexiness between them? Will, the mega record producer, Luke, the mysterious bar owner, Cash, the hottest bad boy to hit the music scene in a long time, and Gavin, the quiet powerhouse attorney. And let's not forget that one interview they all did together a few months ago. Remember how hot they looked?"

"Who looked hot?"

Eleanor stepped onto the patio with a tray of strawberry tarts and placed it on the table beneath the umbrella.

"I love hot men," she stated as she took a seat next to Hannah.

"We were talking about the Sutherland brothers," Hallie explained.

"Oh, yes." Eleanor reached for a tart. "If I was younger, you can bet I'd be going after one of those hunks."

Hannah couldn't help but laugh. Her grandmother had been happily married for decades, but the woman wasn't dead or blind. She was, however, honest and blunt. That must be where Hannah and Hallie had gotten that personality trait.

"Well, I'm not looking for romance," Hannah amended. "I'm looking to take my career to the next level."

Her gram laughed. "Honey, don't lie. You can admit you're attracted to your producer."

"Gram, I don't have time for such nonsense," Hannah insisted with a laugh she hoped sounded convincing. "I'm pushing forward with new material and I want my fans to love it."

"Hallie tells me your first single will be one of Cash's songs," Gram stated as she bit into her tart. "I can't wait to hear it. You two are going to sell out every venue once you start your tour. How many interviews have you scheduled?"

"I'm leaving that to Hallie," Hannah said. "I'm not ready for the press quite yet. Cash and I just had our first session together, but we definitely have chemistry."

"Oh, chemistry." Gram seemed to forget the tart as she set it back on the tray and turned to focus on Hannah. "That sounds fun."

"You know better," Hannah told her. "We have music chemistry, nothing more."

Cash might be sexy and have swagger and twang and a cocky grin, but none of that turned her on the way Will's power and strength did.

And that was *before* she'd slept with him. Now

she couldn't even zero in on how she felt or what she needed. All she knew was she wanted to be with him again and she wanted more time to explore that lean, hard body of his.

He'd not gotten back to her on that, though. She'd told him to think about it and he'd hesitated. Probably a wise reaction on his part, but it didn't keep her from wanting to strip him down and remind him exactly what they'd started…because they weren't done.

"Do you like the song Cash wrote?"

Gram's question pulled Hannah back to the present. She focused on her beautiful grandmother, who still looked like a superstar even though she wasn't wearing a stitch of makeup and she'd pulled her dyed blond hair up on top of her head with just a few pins. The woman was stunning and the world loved her. Hannah only hoped to be in her grandmother's league one day.

"I love the song," Hannah said. "I don't necessarily want it as my first single for my first record with Elite, but we've butted heads a little over that and I'm going to have to concede."

"That's what the contracts are for," Hallie reminded her.

"Yes, yes, I know." Hannah waved her hand to dismiss the obvious. "I might have just suggested something else when we met the other day."

"You can't change things this late in the game," Gram laughed. "Darling, you know that. Your record is due to come out in just a few months."

Yeah, that's what had her stressed. She hadn't recorded one song and she was crunched for time between working on the tour, getting her new look ready for the photo shoot, and preparing for an awards ceremony coming up…not to mention that her emotions were spiraling out of control…

Really, the list felt endless and once she ticked off all those boxes, she was sure she'd have something else to stress over.

All she could do at this point was smile and wave. She knew no other life and she wouldn't trade hers for anything. Hannah was blessed to be in this position. She hadn't gotten here only by being Eleanor Banks's granddaughter. She'd gotten here because she was a damn good singer and worked her ass off just like every other performer who chased the dream.

"What are you wearing for the awards show?" Hannah asked her gram, trying to dodge the topic of Will and his brothers.

"I had Dominic design a short green dress with one sleeve and the other shoulder bare. It's got all the bling and he's getting some killer shoes and jewelry to make me stand out."

As if Eleanor wouldn't stand out on the stage, anyway.

"What about Mags's fundraiser?" Hannah asked. "Are you going?"

Eleanor rolled her eyes and laughed. "Of course I'm going. The media expects it and you know she'll have every tabloid there to get plenty of pictures of her and her good deed."

The rift between Eleanor and Mags had been in the press for decades. The two cohabitated in the same lakeside community and dodged each other as much as possible. But there were always those times when public appearances called for smiles and air kisses, in which case the two would fake it for the camera.

"I have a sexy, sparkly, black low-cut suit I was thinking of wearing," Hannah stated. "Of course, I have that white strapless dress, too."

The dress that had apparently been Will's breaking point. She wouldn't mind giving him another dose of sexy to remind him how damn good they were together.

"The white dress you considered for the photo shoot?" Hallie asked.

Hannah nodded. "I'm thinking about it. I figure everyone will wear black and who knows what Mags will wear."

"Something to get attention, no doubt," Hallie muttered.

"So we're all going?" Hannah asked, glancing to her family.

"Looks like it," Hallie stated. "The town does need funds raised for the rebuild and Beaumont Bay has all the people who can make a big difference."

"And Mags knows that's what will get people there," Eleanor stated. "We'd look heartless if we didn't attend and contribute, though I don't like how she does charity for the show of it and to fish for compliments."

That was another reason the public loved the Banks family. Hannah wasn't being vain or conceited in admitting that they were well-loved because they didn't flash around their charity as a show for the cameras. They often donated privately or under an alias. That's what helping others should be about—just helping, not to get something in return.

Hannah reached for the bottle of wine, poured just a bit more, and then took a drink.

"Can we talk about those Sutherland boys again?" Eleanor asked with a twinkle in her eye. "I have a feeling they're going to be a big influence in the Banks family."

Hannah nearly choked on her pinot. There was no doubt in her mind at least one of those Sutherland boys was going to be a big influence because he'd ruined her for any other sexual partner and all they'd had was a quickie on her studio floor.

She hadn't been entirely joking when she'd told him she would sing about their encounter—she just had to find the right words. And perhaps another session alone with Will would help inspire her.

Ten

"Are you sure this is a good idea?"

Hannah stood just behind the stage at Cheshire, Luke's rooftop bar, with Cash at her side. Hallie and Will were both in agreement that this was a smart move, but Hannah still had reservations.

"Where better to practice that duet you two wanted to use for the tour than right here?" Will asked. "Nobody knows it yet, we can get a good feel for how it will be received, and if you mess anything up, nobody will ever know."

All of those were valid points, but her issue was they'd only practiced it twice. Granted they hadn't done too badly at all, but still. Hannah preferred perfection.

"They're all going to love it," Hallie assured her with a soft smile.

Hannah rested her hand on her guitar and nodded. "I'm sure they will. It's a great song."

Luke had advertised there would be a special guest and announced tickets on sale a week ago. It was last-minute, but that was the nature of the industry at times. That sense of excited urgency had tickets sold out within minutes because everyone knew if Luke had a special guest, that guest was going to be good. Hannah had actually sung here a couple years ago as a pop-in guest.

"All right," she conceded. "If everyone is so confident, then I am, too."

Will continued to stare at her with that heavy gaze and she didn't miss the muscle ticking in his jaw. He was either turned on, irritated, or frustrated...and if he'd felt anything like she had over the last week, since they'd had sex, he was all of the above.

When she'd gotten ready for the evening, she might have taken a little extra time in choosing the perfect outfit to hopefully grab his attention once again.

Nothing would be as attention-grabbing as the strapless dress, but this flirty little sundress with a sweetheart neckline and a ruffle hem paired with her cowgirl boots was fun and sexy. Perfect for the vibe of the bar and to get under Will's skin.

"Ready for me to introduce you?" Luke asked.

"Let's do it," Cash said.

Luke glanced to Hannah and she nodded. "I'm ready."

Moments later, Luke stepped out onto the stage and hyped up the already rowdy crowd. Hannah loved this part of the business. There was nothing like doing small shows. They were more intimate and reminded her of her roots, when she'd first started singing around town hoping someone would notice her for her voice and style and not because of the Banks name.

Luke kept chatting, the sound from the mic echoing behind the rooftop stage.

"Hey."

Hannah turned at Will's low tone.

"You got this," he assured her.

Hannah stared at him, wondering if he always boosted the morale of his artists or if he was comforting her because of what they'd shared. They'd still not discussed that evening—or maybe having a second one—and it was driving her out of her mind.

But right now she had a crowd to charm and her personal life would have to take a back seat.

When Luke announced their names, the crowd went absolutely wild.

"Go kill it," Will told her.

He didn't offer a smile, but that wasn't Will. He was serious all the time. Even during their intimacy, he'd been so damn serious.

Hannah shook the thought from her mind and headed onto the stage with Cash. She'd sworn she wouldn't let her need for Will interfere with her work and that was already turning out to be a lie.

"They're damn good together," Luke commented.

Will couldn't deny the onstage chemistry between his brother and Hannah. This was exactly what he'd wanted when he'd signed her. He'd known they would sound amazing together.

What he hadn't planned on was being jealous of his own brother.

"You okay?"

Will jerked his attention to Luke and nodded. "Just a lot on my mind right now."

"How's the studio coming along?"

Sure, the studio. That's what he should be worried about, but instead he was worried about the fact that he'd slept with his latest artist. Not only did he sleep with her, but he also enjoyed the hell out of it and wanted more.

"It's getting there," Will stated. "I'm anxious to get back into it."

Then he wouldn't be tempted by memories every time he entered Hannah's studio.

"Some people weren't as lucky as we were with that storm," Luke commented as he kept watching the stage.

"No, they weren't."

People had lost homes and others had lost their small businesses, and that was the sole reason Will was going to the charity event at Mags's house. He couldn't care less about her showy lifestyle, but he did want to help rebuild his beautiful town.

Hannah went on to sing one of her older songs, which the crowd also loved. Cash remained on a stool in the background until Hannah was done. Then she really turned on the charm when she started the crowd chanting Cash's name and begging him to play something he'd written that hadn't been heard before. Of course, this had all been discussed beforehand, but it seemed like the crowd really loved this duo.

Will had confidence that once they started their tour, the sellouts would be epic. Maybe they'd even have to add more tour dates, which was every artist's hope.

"Maybe we can talk them in to making this a regular spot," Luke said. "Or do I need to bribe you for that?"

"I'll talk to Hallie and we'll see what we can come up with," Will promised.

Luke glanced to the sister in question, who ended up going out into the crowd and having a drink, but she still remained a little to the side as if ready to hide behind the scenes again.

"She's definitely different from Hannah," Luke commented. "Sweet girl, though."

Will glanced to his brother. "Hands off the Banks sisters."

Holding his hands up in mock surrender, Luke laughed. "Just making a statement. You sound territorial. Has one of the ladies piqued your interest?"

His interest? More like his libido and his raging hormones.

"I'm just laying it out there that my singer and her manager are off-limits."

Luke dropped his hands, but kept the smirk. "Oh, man. Can't wait to see how this plays out," he muttered.

Will was not taking that bait. He remained silent as Cash finished and the two performers waved to the crowd and promised to return one day. Cash even joked about knowing the owner.

As they came off the stage, Hallie joined them. Hannah pulled her guitar strap over her head and held on to the neck of the instrument.

"That was awesome," Hannah exclaimed as she turned to Cash. "You killed it."

"We killed it," he countered before looking to Luke. "Hope that wasn't too presumptuous of me to tell them Hannah and I would be back sometime."

"Not at all. Will and I were just discussing that."

One of the waitstaff brought over a tray of drinks and handed them out. Hannah reached for a glass of water and took a heavy gulp.

Will couldn't tear his eyes away. She was so damn stunning and he wanted to get her alone again. No, it wasn't smart, but a week had passed. He'd thought if he waited, his wants would disappear. Instead, he was more sexually frustrated than ever.

"I'd say the duet was a hit, too," Hallie said. "It was perfect just the way you two did it tonight."

"I agree," Hannah said, tucking her hair behind her ear.

The warm spring breeze swept over the rooftop and Will still couldn't pull his gaze away from the way Hannah's hair danced around her shoulders.

"I'm glad we did this," Cash said as he held on to his beer mug. "Just a little teaser for the big things coming down the pike."

"Can I get you something to eat or something other than water?" Luke asked Hannah.

"No, no. I'm good. I'm going to head home and pour myself a drink and relax on my patio." She finished her water and sighed. "This was a really great night. Thanks for having us."

"Well, you hadn't been here in years, so it was definitely time," Luke told her.

"Past time," she agreed.

When her eyes landed on him, Will pulled himself together.

"I need to discuss something with you," he told her. "I'll walk you out the back way."

Her eyes widened a fraction before she nodded. "Of course."

They said their goodbyes and Will led Hannah to the service elevator that only very few staff used.

The moment they were in and the doors closed, Will turned to Hannah, gripped her face, and kissed her. He backed her to the corner of the elevator and swallowed her gasp. He needed her. He couldn't stand it another second.

Hannah gripped his shoulders and returned the kiss. Apparently she'd been holding in her passion for the last seven days as well.

The elevator chimed and Will moved away. Hannah's red lips were now smeared and there was no denying what she had been doing in the twenty-second elevator ride.

"Will," she whispered just as the doors slid open.

He fisted his hands at his sides to keep from reaching for her again.

"What did you want to talk about?" she asked, staring up at him.

When no one entered, he reached around and pushed the close-door button so they would remain on the main floor and not get interrupted.

"Hell, I don't know," he admitted. "I just couldn't stand it another second."

"Stand what?" She took a half step forward to meet him. "Being near me?" Then she reached up and trailed her fingertips over his lips. "Because I've dreamed of kissing and touching you since you left the other night."

His entire body tightened and he released the button. The doors slid open once again and Will wanted too damn bad to take her hand and haul her out of here, but people would see them and that was the last thing either of them needed.

"Follow me," he demanded as he stepped out, held the door and waited for her.

Hannah moved out of the elevator and waited,

then fell into step beside him as he made his way through the back entrance of The Beaumont. He'd parked his black SUV in the usual spot, near the back door. They worked their way through the hallways where the offices were located, so they really didn't pass anyone. When they got to the door, Will held up a hand.

"Let me make sure nobody is out here," he told her. "We don't need a picture of us getting in my car together and leaving."

"Where are we going?"

Will glanced over his shoulder and met her gaze. "You're coming home with me."

Eleven

Anticipation rolled through Hannah as she waited on Will to come around and open her door. He'd pulled into the garage of his home on the lake and Hannah knew full well why he'd brought her here. Her body was still zinging from that all-too-brief elevator ride.

Not to mention she was always revved up on adrenaline after any show, no matter how big or small. There was also a storm brewing outside. Fat raindrops had hit the vehicle the entire drive here. Hannah had tried to focus on the windshield wipers' pattern instead of her beating heart or her imagination running wild. She didn't fully know what to expect, other than the obvious, but what else was Will wanting from this encounter? Did he want anything more than just the physical aspect? Were they rushing this connection too fast? Was this all a colossal mistake?

Her career couldn't take a hit right now, not with everything on the line with her new look, new sound and new label. And there was no way she'd go back to Cheating Hearts.

Could she be losing control? If she continued this fling, would she be able to stay in charge here? Could she put aside all of her professional concerns and just enjoy herself? Living in the now wasn't something she gave herself the luxury of doing very often.

Maybe she could keep herself in check. Maybe she and Will could pull this off together.

As soon as the door opened, Hannah slid out and found herself plastered against the side of the vehicle and his mouth on hers once again.

Oh, she'd needed this. She'd thought about his mouth, his body, over the last seven days and she knew she hadn't just imagined how mind-blowing he'd been, but she loved having this reminder.

Hannah gripped his shoulders and opened to him. She went up onto her tiptoes to get closer, to have better access.

Stripping him down in his garage was even less classy than seducing him on her studio floor. Surely she could wait and do this properly this time, right? He had to have been thinking about them being together again or he wouldn't have brought her here… unless he'd gotten so turned on during her performance he'd just snapped. In which case, that was just as sexy.

Will eased back, but didn't move away.

"You told me to think about this," he murmured against her lips. "I'm done thinking."

"It's about time."

He kissed her again, but just for a second, then he took her hand and led her through his home. She was sure he had stunning views of the lake and exquisite decor, but right now all she cared about was the bedroom, or whatever room he was leading her to, because her dress and panties were about to melt off.

"Do you think anyone knows where we are or that we left together?" she asked as she followed him up the curved staircase.

As they walked, soft, glowing lights would kick on as they approached, lighting up their path. Once they reached the landing, a flash of lightning lit up the two-story windows and she jumped.

"Easy," he assured her, resting his hands on her shoulders. "You're safe here."

In the lion's den?

"I guess I'm just jumpy after that last storm," she admitted.

Will stepped closer and ran his hands down her arms, then slid them around her waist. "Then stay here for the night."

For the entire night? That was much more intimate than just sex.

"Will, I—"

He covered her mouth with his and lifted her up off the floor. His arms banded around her, just below her backside, and she couldn't stop herself from wrapping her arms around his neck and holding on for the kiss.

"I want to take my time with you," he murmured against her lips. "I want you in my bed and not on the floor. Stay."

Oh, how could she argue with this man? She wanted everything he'd just laid out, and the tender, yet commanding way he spoke to her had her melting.

He shouldn't be throwing romance into this. She didn't want romance. She didn't have time for romance.

Yet she couldn't help but admit that she hadn't had anyone even *try* to romance her in so long… Maybe that's what she was afraid of.

"Now you're the one thinking too much," he whispered as he eased her back. "Don't overthink this, Hannah. It's just us. Nobody knows."

Nobody knows. Right. And that's what brought her attention back to the physical. There was nothing more going on here and she needed to get out of her head and into the moment.

Hannah stepped back and toed off her boots. When she reached for the strap of her dress, Will covered her hand.

"Don't rob this from me again."

His throaty command sent another bolt of arousal

through her. With the soft glow from the lighting along the steps and the sconces on the wall around the windows, she could make out that fiery passion staring back at her.

Without any warning, Will bent down and lifted her into his arms, with one arm behind her back and the other behind her knees. He turned and started up the next set of steps to the second floor.

Damn it. He was putting romance into this fling. When they were in her studio everything had been fast and frantic and exhilarating. She hadn't had much time to think of anything other than the fact she was finally getting what she wanted.

But now? Well, now she was liking this version a little too much. Which was how she found herself looping her arms around his neck and resting her head against his shoulder.

"I can walk you know."

"Oh, I'm aware. I've watched those sexy, swaying hips for too damn long now." He reached the top of the stairs and glanced down to her. "And I know you wore this dress to drive me crazy."

"It worked," she laughed.

"You're a minx."

"Thank you."

Will continued down the dimly lit hall and turned into a room she assumed was his. How many other women had he whisked up here Rhett Butler-style?

A surge of jealousy threatened to overtake her, so Hannah had to remind herself this wasn't an actual relationship and Will wasn't a saint. Neither was she. Of course, they'd both had lovers before now, but she sure as hell didn't want those thoughts interrupting this moment.

When he crossed the room and came to the edge of the bed, Will eased her down, making sure her entire body slid deliciously against his on the way down.

The material of the dress bunched between them, leaving her bottom half exposed. Will wasted no time in reaching for her hips, hooking his thumbs in the waistband of her panties, and jerking them down to her thighs. Hannah assisted by shimmying until they fell to the floor and then she kicked them aside.

Will gripped her bare backside and Hannah instinctively pressed her pelvis to his.

"We can't wait seven days again," he growled into her ear. "I'm trying to take my time."

"Don't try so hard," she demanded. "Just take what you want."

With a groan or growl, she wasn't sure which, Will gathered the material of her dress and yanked it up and over her head, leaving her completely bare.

"No bra?" he asked.

This was where Hannah struggled a little with her confidence. She shrugged, hoping her self-pity didn't ruin anything.

"I wasn't blessed in that area, so I don't always wear one. Nobody can tell."

Will glanced down, reached for her hands and

held them out wide. He took a step back, still holding her arms out.

"I don't know who planted that seed in your head, but you're damn perfect from where I'm standing."

Oh, no. No, no, no. He couldn't say things like that and expect her to keep her heart closed off. Hearing pretty words, the *perfect words*, murmured during a passionate moment felt more intimate to her than using the infamous *L* word.

Before she could reply, Will covered her breasts with his palms and stepped back in.

"Perfect," he whispered once again before sliding his lips across hers.

Hannah fully believed him. He wasn't saying that just to have her—he'd already had her and clearly he wanted more. Something about this man made her feel worshipped, cherished…special.

She'd put personal relationships on the back burner for a few years. Getting involved with anyone was so risky and never private in her world. Maybe she was just letting her mind get too deep into this because she'd been alone for too long.

Or maybe there was a kernel of something more than sex here. If that was the case, they were both in deep trouble.

Will slid his hands down the dip in her waist and lifted her enough to set her on the edge of the bed. Then he braced his hands on either side of her hips and held his mouth close to hers.

"You're staying here," he told her. "There's too much I want to do and it's getting nasty out."

Hannah nodded. There was no way she would argue and no way she wanted to be anywhere else. Finding herself in Will's bedroom was much more than she'd bargained for when she first knew she wanted him. She thought they'd have a one-and-done and then be out of each other's systems.

Yet here they were and he wanted her to spend the night. Even though a week had passed, this intimate relationship was progressing rapidly. The fact she even thought of any of this using the word *relationship* should have had her running out of this house...

"I'll stay," she agreed.

Will exhaled as if he'd been waiting for her to agree to his terms. She didn't know what she was actually getting into, but right now she couldn't worry about that. They'd already crossed the line, so she might as well enjoy herself.

"Why are you still dressed?" she asked, reaching for his belt buckle.

"I'm waiting on you to strip me."

Will took a step back and held her gaze as if to challenge her. He didn't know her that well—she rarely turned down a risk that would have amazing benefits. Taking off Will's clothes was the equivalent of having extra whipped cream on top of a sundae. Nobody would say no to that.

Hannah came to her feet and immediately went to work. She yanked the belt from the loops and flung it aside. Then she reached for the top button of his dress shirt and slid it through the tiny hole. One after another, she traveled down the straight path until she had that broad, bare chest on display for her enjoyment.

She flattened her palms against his torso, relishing the fact that he had to take in a deep breath. Knowing her touch affected him so strongly was extremely useful information to have. She had him just as revved up and turned on as she was—it was really only fair. She'd been dreaming of him for seven days, for longer… Texts and phone calls came and went and he'd still never mentioned a thing.

Thankfully he'd finally come to his senses in that elevator.

Hannah eased her hands up and over his chest until she reached his shoulders. She gently shoved the shirt down Will's arms until it fell to the floor.

"If my chest looked like yours, I'd never wear a shirt," she told him.

He chuckled. "If your chest looked like mine, you wouldn't be here. But, hey, feel free to go topless anytime. I rather enjoy the view."

Men were such simple creatures with simple needs, but there was something not so simple about Will that fascinated her, amused her, at times grated on her last nerve, but damn it, she couldn't pull herself away from him…at least not personally.

She reached for the snap on his jeans and carefully slid them down his legs. He helped by kicking off his boots and then stood before her wearing nothing but boxer briefs and a naughty grin.

The man rarely smiled, but now… Hannah shivered knowing she was in for one hell of a night.

"You should do that more often." She reached up and slid her fingertip over his lips. "Smiling is sexy on you."

He nipped at her finger then removed his briefs. "I smile all the time."

"Rarely."

"Not during work."

In a swift move, Will lifted her once again and tossed her onto the bed before following her down and hovering over her.

"We're not working for the rest of the night," he promised with a low growl. "And I'm done talking altogether."

He wrapped an arm between her and the mattress, then flipped them both until she was straddling his lap. Hannah couldn't help but laugh, and caught herself by flattening her hands on his chest.

"When you decide you want something, you really move fast," she told him.

He gripped her hips. "This past week didn't feel like it went fast."

Hannah eased up onto her knees to align their bodies. "That's your fault. You took too long to think about this."

Will groaned as she rubbed herself against him and curled her fingertips slightly against his skin.

"I can admit when I'm wrong," he growled between gritted teeth. "Which is why you'll be staying the night. I need more."

With that, he jerked her hips down until their bodies joined. Hannah cried out and arched instantly at the sensations flooding her.

He reached up to cup her breasts. The strength and warmth of his large hands turned her on even more. She pressed into him, needing everything he was willing to give. He'd clearly put her on top to give her control here, which was just another one of Will's traits that she couldn't help but lo—

No. Mercy, how did that word almost creep into her head?

She eased down, resting her hands on either side of his head, and covered his lips with hers. Will gripped her backside and took over the momentum.

Maybe he hadn't been relinquishing control.

The silent way he commanded her body had her climbing higher and higher. There was no holding back her release, but she wanted to see him…and she wanted him to see her.

Hannah sat back up and worked her hips as she pressed her hands against his chest. When her eyes met his, she saw something she didn't recognize. What did he see when he looked at her?

But before she could contemplate it, her body let go and all thoughts vanished. Hannah cried out. Her eyes shut as if she could hold on to this moment, this sensation, forever.

With his hands still on her rear, Will jerked his hips faster, harder, until his body followed hers. He took one hand and curled his fingers behind her neck to pull her down.

Once again she opened her mouth for him, her body still zinging from all of their delicious activities.

Will seemed to settle beneath her and Hannah eased from the kiss to rest her forehead against his. She didn't know what to say. She hadn't ever stayed all night with a man she wasn't dating, so she wasn't sure what the protocol was here.

But she needn't have worried. As per usual, Will took over. He settled her to his side, pulled the comforter around them, and kissed her forehead.

Everything about this seemed so intimate, much more intimate than the sex itself.

With the storm raging outside, Hannah couldn't help but wonder if she should write a song about the storm raging within when a woman wanted a forbidden man.

Twelve

"It's not often I eat cold pizza in bed at three in the morning," Hannah joked.

Will wanted to swipe this pizza out of the way and remove the dress shirt of his that Hannah had put on. They'd fallen asleep to the storm and had woken up about a half hour ago with growling stomachs. As soon as he learned Hannah hadn't had dinner because she'd been too excited about the performance, he'd grabbed the one thing he didn't have to cook.

"You don't like cold pizza?" he asked.

"Oh, I love all pizza," she corrected. "Cold, hot, room temperature. Any toppings, any crust. I literally think pizza is the greatest food."

"That's good to know for the future."

Hannah tipped her head, sending her bed-messed

hair falling over one shoulder. "The future? Are you taking me on a date or something?"

When she laughed, he realized how ridiculous he'd sounded. For a split second he had lost his damn mind and actually thought about taking her out. That wasn't even possible and he wasn't shopping for a girlfriend.

Not only that, attempting to "date," or have a relationship with his newest artist, would be detrimental to his label, not to mention to all of the artists who trusted him to keep a solid reputation. There was too much at stake and he couldn't take such a risk. What they had—it had to stay a secret.

Could everything be just fine if they proceeded as they had been? Sure. But could it all blow up in their faces? Absolutely.

"Maybe I want to make sure I have enough on hand when you spend the night again."

Her eyes darted down to her lap for a moment, then back up. She sighed and seemed to be rolling thoughts through her mind.

"Are we going to keep doing this?" she finally asked.

"Why wouldn't we?" he countered.

Now he did pick up the box and turned to set it on the nightstand. Will scooted closer to her, gripped her legs, and pulled her until her legs were overlapping his thighs.

"We both enjoy this." He rested his hands on that perfect crease between her thigh and her hip. "Nobody knows what we're doing and we seem to get along better this way. We're not butting heads like we were in the beginning."

Her smile sent another punch of arousal through him. "That was just the sexual tension."

"Or the fact that you and Hallie play twin games."

Hannah tapped her fingertip to his chin, then trailed down until she got to his chest. Her hands started exploring. It seemed he still hadn't fully calmed down from their first session. How could he want a woman with such a fierceness? How could he not even put his emotions into words?

"We don't play games," Hannah murmured. "We just have each other's backs."

Will wrapped his arms around her and pulled her even closer until his mouth was a breath from hers.

"I don't know how I ever confused the two of you." He slid his mouth across hers, back and forth. "You might look the same, but you're different. You're..."

Mine.

"You get to me," he added.

No way in hell was he going to claim her. If he went down that path, they'd be on shaky ground. Making this public... The timing—with her just signing with Elite—would put a dark cloud over her career, and his, and people would wonder if Hannah had slept with him to get what she wanted.

Will would cut ties with her before he ever saw

her or her career damaged. He cared for Hannah, maybe more than he wanted to admit.

She looped her arms around his head. "You get to me, too," she confessed with a light kiss. "And I'm all for a closed-door fling."

Closed-door fling. That sounded so dirty and classless. But that's exactly what he'd laid out in his mind, right? That's exactly what they'd have to do if he wanted to protect Hannah and Elite. While he cared for her reputation, he also had to look out for his own label.

Will didn't want to talk anymore and he didn't want to make rules or worry about anything else. All he wanted was Hannah. She was in his bed and he fully intended to take advantage of their time together, because once her record was released and she started touring, their alone time would be minimal and he would have to share her with the world.

She slid a fingertip between his eyebrows. "Why so serious again?"

He snagged her finger and kissed the tip. "I'm thinking of where I want you next."

Her body trembled against his. That's all he wanted—having Hannah just as aroused and ready as he was.

"You want to see my oversized shower?" he offered with a grin. "There's a one-way window that overlooks the lake, but nobody can see in. I wouldn't mind having you in the moonlight."

Her lids fluttered closed and she pulled in a breath. "I can't resist you and your sexy words."

Will maneuvered them off the bed and carried her to his bathroom. "That's what I'm counting on."

Walking through the new studio was quite exhilarating. Will was impressed with how far things had come in such a short time. His contractors had left for the day, he'd taken Hannah back to her car early this morning, and now he was just getting some quiet time in the place that was like his second home.

He was taking in all the new features and already planning how to get his artists in here to start working. Even so, Will couldn't get Hannah out of his mind. Having her stay at his house last night had probably not been the smartest move, but he couldn't exactly change what happened. He wasn't sorry *any* of this had happened, but he did need to be smart about it. He needed to protect Hannah and Elite.

There was a tap on the front door and Will turned his attention to the hallway. He had no idea who would be knocking, but he headed toward the entry.

Will caught sight of a familiar fake smile and bling. Nothing like wanting to be alone and then getting interrupted by Mags Dumond.

He flicked the lock on the door and pushed it open to allow her inside.

"What brings you by, Margaret?" he asked.

That wide, red-lipped smiled faltered just a touch

before she replied. "You know I hate that name. Mags, Will. Everyone calls me Mags."

Yeah, he knew that, but grating on her nerves was too easy and too damn fun. Besides, now that he had her top star, Will knew she was a bit more annoyed with him and very likely much more stressed overall.

While Elite had historically produced country legends, it was Cheating Hearts Records who'd taken the limelight over the last few decades. But Will's ownership of Elite was changing all that, and now he had Hannah, who'd been Mags's big-ticket star.

"So what brings you by?" Will asked again.

"Well, I saw your car outside and knew you were renovating." She bypassed him and started her own self-guided tour. "I just wanted to see how things were coming along."

More like you wanted to snoop on the competition.

Will turned and stared at her back as she continued to glance around. He had to admit the waiting area had turned out a hell of a lot nicer than he'd envisioned. He'd gone with classic white and dark wood. He had black-and-white images on the wall of various artists who'd sung for Elite in the past and that he'd personally produced. In the corner sat a piano that had been used by Ray Charles. Lining the hallway leading to the recording studio, Will had hung a variety of guitars used by famous stars.

One of his favorite parts about the country music

industry was the history, the dreamers who'd taken a chance on what they wanted.

An annoying niggle crept up in his thoughts. He'd become a dreamer since Hannah. An erotic dreamer, but whatever. He wanted her and was going after her, but to what end? Would they just have sex until they were ready to move on? Until they were out of each other's systems? Would that ever happen? Or would she move on and want to date someone?

That instant image had a spear of jealousy stabbing him. Will didn't like that idea one bit. Because that likely meant another man would be in her bed and Will refused to even let that image sink in.

"This is all lovely," Mags said as she turned back around.

Will cleared his thoughts of Hannah. "It is," he agreed. "Is that all you needed?"

Mags laughed. "Oh, Will. No need to be in such a hurry to get me to leave. I also haven't received your RSVP for my charity ball."

That would be because he was too busy keeping Hannah naked and satisfied, but he'd certainly be keeping that information to himself.

"Must've slipped my mind with all the work I've been doing," he replied. "I'll be there."

The front door opened behind him and Will turned to see his brother Gavin stepping through. Perfect timing. Will could use an excuse to get Mags out of there. The woman was only here to snoop. Will couldn't believe she hadn't brought up Hannah yet, but thankfully his brother might have interrupted before she could broach the subject.

"Am I interrupting?" Gavin asked.

"Not at all," Will told him. "Mags was getting ready to go. I believe our business is done. Unless you want to discuss something else?"

"Oh, we can talk at the party," she assured him. "Please, tell Hannah I miss her, and I can't wait to catch up when she's at my house."

Will nodded and waited as Mags let herself out. Once the door closed behind her, he turned to his brother. "I wasn't expecting you, but I've never been happier for your visit."

Gavin laughed and held up a folder. "Well, I was on my way to your house when I saw your car here. I have those contracts you need to sign regarding the promotional events you have planned over the summer with Hannah and Cash."

"Everything look squared away?" he asked.

There was nobody else Will would trust more to be his attorney than his brother. Gavin was savvy and powerful. He was the most sought-out attorney in the industry, but Will and Elite always took top priority.

"It's all in order," Gavin stated, handing over the file. "I put tabs where you need to sign. Just get them back to me by the end of the week and I'll take it from there."

Will nodded. "I assume you RSVP'd to Mags's event?"

"I did. I can't imagine anyone not attending since the funds are going to rebuild."

"Are you bringing a date?" Will asked.

Gavin shrugged. "Hadn't thought much about it."

"Well, it's pretty soon."

"I might bring someone," Gavin added. "I haven't had time to date much lately, but since this will be a popular event, I'm sure I could find someone to take."

Gavin liked to date, but he was discreet about his activities. He'd always been known as the quiet, reserved Sutherland brother, but for reasons Will never understood, that was appealing to some women.

"You going with Hannah?" Gavin asked.

"What do you mean?"

Gavin's eyebrows rose. "Relax." He laughed. "Just asking if you were going as a united front. You know, since she's new with Elite and just left Cheating Hearts. What did you think I meant?"

Will cursed beneath his breath. He needed to chill out and relax or everyone would be able to tell he had a thing with Hannah. Not that he didn't trust his brothers implicitly, but he and Hannah had agreed to keep their intimacy between them. He respected her too damn much to go back on that.

"I just didn't want you to think we were going as a date," Will joked. "Wouldn't want anyone to get the wrong impression."

"I doubt anyone would think that," Gavin replied. "Unless you're actually dating."

Will stared at his brother and Gavin narrowed his eyes. "You're dating?"

"What? Hell no, we're not dating."

Will and Hannah never got out of the bedroom so there was no time for dating. Technically his response wasn't a lie. Surely his attorney brother would appreciate that logic.

"You hesitated, so I didn't know if something was going on." Gavin shifted his stance and crossed his arms, holding Will in place with that lawyer stare. "You know if something is going on, you can tell me. I'd understand. She's an attractive woman. Though, I have to say, if something *is* going on, it's not the smartest move on your part."

Gavin did that a lot. He'd argue with himself and give both sides. Must be an occupational hazard.

"There's nothing to tell," Will responded, trying to reassure him. "I'll get these papers signed and to you tomorrow."

He hated the guilt that crept in. Now he was lying, and he never lied to his family. They meant too much to him. At the end of the day, if everything else was stripped away from his life, Will would still have his brothers.

Once Gavin left, Will remained behind and glanced over the documents, but his mind was back on Hannah and the fact that he'd just now put her above his loyalty to his brother.

And that right there told him that this—whatever it was—was about more than sex. He had no idea what to do now or how to handle it, but he was definitely going to have to figure out where the hell his head was in all of this. He refused to ruin his relationships with his family.

Did he want more with Hannah?

Damn…he did.

He wasn't sure to what extent, but he wanted more than sex. There was such a fine line here and he was in unfamiliar territory. Not to mention, he didn't know exactly where Hannah stood.

Will knew one thing, though. He always got what he wanted and he never settled.

There had to be a way around all of this.

Now if he could just figure out exactly what he wanted, then he could figure out what he should do about this personal thing he now seemed to have with Hannah.

Thirteen

Hannah sat out on her dock with her guitar. The evening was her favorite time because she could unwind and relax so long as she didn't have any engagements. Once she and Cash started touring, there wouldn't be much down time or evenings spent on the lake.

There were only a couple boats out on the water. Every now and then Hannah would glance up and see someone she knew and offer a wave. No way would she want to be anywhere else than Beaumont Bay. This was the most relaxed place to live and work.

She didn't bring her notebook out with her. She'd opted just to work on the new material with only her guitar. Sometimes getting back to the basics before building and layering was the best exercise for her vocal chords and mentality.

The cell at her side vibrated against the wooden dock and Hannah stopped to glance at the screen.

You look sexy

Will's text had her smiling and glancing out to the water. Sure enough, there he was on his boat. He didn't wave and she didn't, either. As far as anyone was concerned, they only had a working relationship.

But she hadn't been with him in a couple days and she was getting cranky.

She grabbed her phone and shot off a reply.

Sex on a boat sounds fun and private

It didn't take long for his comeback to pop on the screen.

Maybe you can sneak down to my dock when it gets dark

A shiver of excitement ran down her spine. Hannah smiled and told him she'd be there. When she set down her phone, she picked up her guitar and got back to singing, but she couldn't get her mind off the fact that Will could see her. There was something arousing knowing he was watching her and found her sexy. She wanted him to find her attractive, to want to spend more time with her.

They had a physical relationship right now, and a working relationship, but a part of her wanted more.

She wanted to get to know him on a deeper level, to know what made him want to be a producer and get into this industry. She wanted to know about the dynamics between him and his brothers, because they all seemed so powerful in their own ways. They all complemented each other.

But desiring a deeper relationship—a romantic relationship—could ruin her reputation. How would the media spin everything? Negative headlines typically meant more attention and that only spawned even more publicity…and not the kind she or Will needed right now, just as she was reconstructing her career and helping Cash relaunch his.

Maybe they could just keep everything behind closed doors until they figured out how best to handle all of this. Everything was new, the professional and the personal, so this chapter in both their lives would be a delicate one. Each step had to be calculated.

Hannah couldn't wait until night fell. She gathered up her guitar and headed back to the dock and up the stairs toward her home. Maybe she should take a little more care with getting ready for Will. There was a flirty outfit she had in mind that would certainly drive him a little crazy.

As anxious as she was for physical intimacy, she also wanted to dig in to his mind and find out if her feelings were just because of the lust or if there was more.

Because something told her…she was falling for Will Sutherland.

* * *

Will helped Hannah step onto his boat. She wore a little black strapless dress that hugged her chest and flared out just a bit and then stopped just below that delicious ass. One tiny gust of wind and he'd be able to see exactly what panties she'd chosen for the night.

She had on her signature cowgirl boots and her hair was down and curled. She'd lightened up on the makeup and was a little less Hannah the superstar and a little more Hannah, small-town girl.

And damn if he didn't enjoy both.

"This is amazing," she exclaimed as he led her down to the galley. "You have parties on here?"

Will escorted her to the cabin where she could put her bag. "I have thrown a few parties. But tonight, it's a private party."

She dropped her small bag onto his bed and he barely resisted the urge to toss her down and get everything going. He wanted her…bad. Which was nothing new, but he knew he needed to calm down. Obviously, that's why she'd come here, but she'd been on board for all of two minutes. Surely, he could control himself long enough to welcome her.

"What do you say we go up to the aft deck? I have something set up for us near the hot tub."

"Will anyone see us?" she asked.

"It's dark and I only have the dim, deck floor lights on." He reached for her hands and squeezed. "Trust me?"

Hannah smiled. "Of course."

He led her up to the deck and hoped she liked the surprise he'd planned. After seeing her on the dock earlier, he'd put a plan into motion. She'd looked like a dream sitting there with her guitar and her hair blowing in the wind, her bare feet dangling over the edge of the dock. This was the country gal the public loved so much. This was that down-to-earth woman who could relate to her fans. She hadn't had a stitch of bling on and she had looked almost innocent.

"Wow," Hannah exclaimed as she glanced around. "You really went all out—unless you had some chef do all of this."

Will smacked his hand to his chest. "I'm offended that you think I couldn't put this together. It's just some finger foods and wine. Nothing major."

"Well, it looks really nice."

She removed her boots and set them aside, then took a seat on the cushions he'd placed on the floor around their deck picnic. She adjusted her dress around her as Will took a seat next to her.

"Is this a date?" she asked.

Will met her gaze. He really didn't know how to answer. He hadn't thought of the evening in that manner, but now that she was here, enjoying the surprise he'd put together just for her, he easily saw why she'd asked.

Gavin's question about dating Hannah came back to him. Will had vehemently denied that they were dating.

"I'll take your silence to mean you're terrified to answer that," she laughed. "It's okay."

Will reached for the wine from the ice bucket and uncorked it. He poured two glasses while thinking of what to say, but that's when he realized that maybe he did want this to be a date. So what if he did? She didn't seem upset about the idea and he wanted to know the side of Hannah that only her family knew. There was more to this woman who held so much passion for her family, her life, and her career.

He handed her a glass of cabernet. "I respect you, Hannah. I know we have a working relationship and a closed-door relationship, but I don't want you to think that I'm using you for sex."

Hannah swirled her wine and pursed her lips. "I never thought you were using me," she told him. "Do you feel I'm using you?"

Will couldn't help but laugh. "Use me all you want, because I'm having a hell of a time."

Hannah set aside her glass and reached for a napkin and a few cubes of cheese. As she popped one after another into her mouth, she seemed to be mulling something over.

"I wouldn't mind if this was a date," she finally said.

That bold statement made him realize one thing. He wanted that, too.

"Then it's a date."

Hannah's wide smile was so genuine, it hit him straight in the heart.

No. Hearts should not be involved here. There was no time for more than a physical relationship, yet he'd just admitted that this evening was a date. Now he'd gone and crossed another line he could never step back from.

Their journey was progressing at a faster rate than he could keep up with. So long as everything stayed just between them, maybe they could maneuver these uncharted waters together and hopefully keep their reputations, and Elite's, positive and stellar.

"Tell me about your songs."

Hannah's gaze jerked to him. He'd clearly caught her off guard.

"My songs?" she asked.

Will nodded, then grabbed a grape and popped it into his mouth. "Tell me more about what makes you want to be a songwriter and why you're hiding your lyrics."

Hannah pulled in a deep breath and reached for her wine again. "I've always jotted down thoughts. Even before I knew I wanted to be a singer, I'd doodle one-liners or come up with a chorus. I never did much more, but I always had little stories in my heart."

"All songs tell a story."

She nodded. "Exactly. So as I got older, once people realized I could sing and I wasn't just going to get a deal because of my famous grandmother, I would escape from the chaos and write. It became like my therapy, if that makes sense."

Will shifted, crossing his legs so he could face her fully. The soft glow from the trim along the stern and around the hot tub was the perfect lighting. They were out in the open on the dark water, but private.

"Cash says the same," Will said. "He's always been writing and he's damn good. He's done a few songs for other Elite artists. Songwriting takes a special talent. So why haven't your lyrics gone anywhere besides that notebook?"

"Mags wasn't too fond of my stuff," Hannah admitted. "She would always say she was, but then put off letting me record them, saying maybe for the next album. Or she'd try to convince me that maybe I should sell those songs and let someone else do them. But that's not what I wanted, what I want. I'm not writing songs to make money. That's never been the goal. I want to sing my own words from my heart."

Because she was that passionate. There was no denying how amazing a singer Hannah was, but he had no doubt when she sang her own music, there would be a difference.

"Why wouldn't Mags let you?" he asked. "Did you show her your stuff?"

Hannah sighed. "I didn't show her the notebook you saw. I actually wrote out one of my songs, but didn't tell her whose it was. She loved it."

Will slid his hand over her bare knee and stroked his thumb back and forth. He couldn't *not* touch her, especially when she was opening up to him. Hannah was the type of person who wouldn't do that easily and he wanted to be supportive and listen.

"Once I told her it was mine," she went on, "Mags quickly changed her tune. She said my schedule was full and so was my song list. Maybe for the next album. That became the cycle. Anything to keep me from doing my own music. I know she and my grandmother both debuted songs at the same time, and my gram made it bigger. Maybe Mags just thought she could live through me or maybe she was trying to prove to my gram that Mags could make me an even bigger star. I'm not sure."

There was no doubt in his mind that Mags had some hidden agenda where Hannah was concerned. If Hannah had done her own music, likely Mags would've seen that as a shift in who was actually in control.

Will knew how important that was to artists. Cash loved writing and recording his own songs and to have a piece of his creativity stripped away would certainly affect his work. He couldn't imagine what Mags had done to Hannah's spirit. He hadn't thought of that before. When he and Hannah and Hallie all discussed contract negotiations, none of this had been mentioned. Had Hannah been gun-shy? Had she just wanted to get away from Mags and then try again?

"Does Hallie know about this notebook?"

Hannah took another sip of wine and shook her head. "She knows I'd like to do my own music, that's why I ultimately left Mags. But she doesn't know about the notebook that you saw. I didn't intend for anyone to see that until it was completely ready to be presented."

"Yet you showed me."

Hannah laughed. "You stole it and looked without permission."

"Semantics."

"You learn that from your lawyer brother?" she joked with a wide smile.

"Gavin has taught me enough," Will agreed. "We all actually feed off each other, if that makes sense. It's just a special bond."

"I get that. I have a special bond with Hallie, too. Being a twin is something most people don't understand."

Will slid his hand up a little higher, easing beneath the hem of her dress. "Oh, I'm very aware of how you two operate."

Hannah set her glass to the side and inched closer to him, causing his hand to travel farther up her thigh.

"You didn't suffer," she joked. "I'll admit the first time was totally my fault, but at the house when you thought she was me, that was all on you."

Will shook his head. "I have no idea how I could confuse the two of you. The difference is so clear to me now."

"Not many people can tell us apart when I'm not all dressed up in Hannah Banks mode."

His fingertips grazed the edge of her panties at her hip. “I like this Hannah. She’s laid-back, she’s calm, she’s open.”

Hannah tipped her head and kept that killer smile in place. “Opening up to you seems easy. I haven’t found anyone other than Hallie or my gram that I can really talk to.”

And yet he’d seen those lyrics. They were not only close to her heart, but some were also about him. That spoke volumes about where this relationship was headed.

There was so much more here than sex. Intimacy had many different levels and they’d just dug down deeper to the next one. Two weeks ago, a night like this would have scared the hell out of him, but now… Will wasn’t opposed to the idea of seeing where this went.

At the same time, though, they still had to be careful. If the press caught wind of the fact that he was seeing Hannah outside of work, they would speculate as to why she’d signed on with Elite, and they would wonder why Will’s brother was the only opening act for her new tour. Elite and Hannah would have a black mark.

His name and his label’s reputation had been important to him since he’d become the owner. With some of the top names in the industry trusting him, Will refused to let his hormones get in the way of his business.

The burden was his to carry and he had to protect

all parties involved if he couldn't let Hannah go back to being only a professional acquaintance.

"What do you say we take this picnic into my cabin?" he suggested.

Hannah's eyebrows rose. "I think you have the best ideas."

Will guided her toward his cabin, but didn't tell her that he'd never taken a woman in here. He'd had parties on his boat, of course, but nothing wild or out of control. His boat was his escape when he wanted to be alone and he'd never once brought a date back here.

Hannah was special. She was working her way further and further into his personal world. He just had to figure out how far he was willing to let this go, because if he wasn't careful, someone could wind up getting hurt.

Fourteen

"It's absolutely perfect."

Hannah turned from side to side in her floor-length mirror and made sure her white dress was smoothed down, her hair wasn't frizzy, and her makeup was perfect. Hallie had brought in a team to make sure everything was top-notch for the photo shoot today.

But Will wasn't here yet.

He'd texted that he'd gotten caught up with the contractor going over some final details at his studio and would be here as soon as he could break away.

She really shouldn't have butterflies in her stomach. This shoot was just about doing pictures for another magazine. She'd done hundreds in the past. But she'd never done one celebrating women or for anything about inspiring future artists. She'd never done one where she was also trying to relaunch her look and sound. She was nervous and excited and, damn it, she wanted Will by her side.

In the past, she'd wanted Hallie, but lately, she wanted both of the people who were special to her.

So what did that say about the relationship she'd developed with Will? And what did that say about the future? She not only had her career to protect, but she also had her heart.

"Are you happy with how everything turned out?" Hallie asked, meeting Hannah's eyes in the reflection in the mirror.

Hannah nodded. "I think this was the best choice."

They were going with the simple white theme, but some photos would be outside on the dock and some would be inside in the studio. Hannah wanted her fans to see all sides of her. After Will had said he was attracted to both sides of her, she realized her fans likely were, too.

"Are you ready to go downstairs?" Hallie asked. "I believe they are all set up for you."

Hannah had stalled as long as possible, waiting on Will to arrive, but she didn't want to hold up the crew anymore.

She turned to her sister and smiled. "Let's go."

Once they were downstairs, the photographer went over what they had in mind and the specifications from the journalist and the art department from the magazine.

She would start outside on the dock with one of her guitars. Hannah chose the one that her gram had given her when she'd turned twenty-five and won her first major award. Hannah loved this one most of all and her gram would love seeing this in the spread.

Hannah and Hallie escorted the crew out to the dock, where they had already set up their equipment. Hannah lifted the flowy white skirt so as not to drag it over the grass. She'd never worn this dress, but the sexy, down-to-earth, almost boho style really spoke to her and she had a feeling she was going to love these photos more than any others she'd had done.

Which got her mind going in the direction of her new album cover. She and Will hadn't discussed that, but she already had some ideas.

Hannah listened to the photographer, about how he wanted her to pose. She took a seat on the dock and Hallie adjusted the skirt and Hannah's hair. Once everything was in place, Hallie handed over the guitar.

"Perfect," Jim, the photographer, said. "This lighting is so great today and this is an awesome angle."

Hannah glanced out to the lake, then she looked to her guitar. Finally, she shifted her legs to the side and Hallie readjusted her skirt to fan out around her bare feet. When Hannah looked up to Jim to see if this was the right angle, she spotted Will standing in the distance. He hadn't come any closer—he remained about halfway down the steps leading to the dock.

He met her gaze and his mouth tipped into a small smile. Hannah's stomach knotted up.

"Hannah. You okay?"

Hallie's question got her attention and Hannah shifted. "I'm good. Is this the right pose?"

"Love it," Jim said as he snapped away. "Look just over my shoulder, but drape your arm over your guitar."

Just over his shoulder was no problem. She stared at Will and he continued to hold her with his eyes. Everything in her settled and she felt…at peace. When they'd first met he'd driven her crazy and she knew she'd grated on his nerves. But now… Now he was much more to her than she'd ever thought he should be.

Hannah couldn't be sorry and she wasn't even going to bother denying that she'd developed feelings for him. She didn't quite know what to do about it, though. If she told him, that could put him in an awkward spot. He'd have to tell her that he didn't… or maybe he did. Either way, if she fully opened up, they would be going even deeper, into an emotional area they probably weren't ready for. All of this was moving much too fast for her and it was entirely too new for her to be making drastic decisions.

"I think we've got enough of those," Jim stated. "How about a few with you leaning against the post here and we can prop your guitar against your hip?"

Hallie and Jim adjusted her and Will stepped on down to the dock.

"Looks like things are going great," he commented.

"She's a natural beauty," Jim replied. "We'll have a difficult time choosing just a few for the article."

"The ones outside are probably going to be my favorite," Hallie chimed in. "Hannah, you are seriously glowing."

Her eyes met Will's once again and he shot her a wink that only she could see. Why did that simple gesture have her stomach in those giddy knots? The man did some of the naughtiest things to her in private, but a wink seemed so intimate.

"She's glowing, all right." Jim held the screen of his camera for Hallie and Will to see. "Look at just a few of the shots I've gotten."

Then he showed Hannah and she had to admit, she hadn't seen anything like these photos before… not with her in them. They were mesmerizing. There was something about them that made her smile and fall in love with her life all over again.

She glanced back up to Will and that's when it hit her. She'd fallen in love with her life because she was *actually in love*.

Jim and Hallie were talking, but Hannah wasn't listening. She could barely hear them for the distracting thought that had just slammed into her. When had she fallen in love with Will? How could she let something like this happen?

Will's gaze met hers and he must've seen something in her eyes, because he drew in his eyebrows and cocked his head in confusion. Yeah, she was confused as hell, too. She didn't have time for love. She wasn't looking for love. And she most definitely couldn't be in love with her producer.

What would people think? That she'd slept her way into a new contract? That she'd only jumped to Elite because she thought she could use her charms to get what she wanted?

None of this would look good for her career, for Will, or for Elite.

"If you want to go get changed, I'll start setting up inside."

Jim's request pulled Hannah back to the moment and away from Will's quizzical stare.

"Sure," she told him with a smile.

Jim started taking down the equipment and Hallie turned to Hannah.

"Are you okay?" she whispered.

"I'm fine."

Hallie placed a hand on her shoulder. "You were glowing moments ago and now you look like you're about to faint. What happened?"

Everything.

"Must be the heat," Hannah replied. "No worries. Let's head in and you can help me get ready for the next setup."

As they started up the steps, Will stopped her.

"Go on ahead," she told Hallie. "I'll be right there."

Hallie glanced between the two of them, but ultimately moved away.

"What's going on?" he asked.

Hannah pasted on her perfected smile. "Nothing. I'm glad you made it."

"Don't do the games, Hannah. I know you too well now." He slid his hand to the inside of her bare arm, just enough to send tingles down her spine. "What happened?"

Mercy, she did love him.

This was going to be an absolute disaster and someone was going to wind up hurt. She couldn't just turn off her feelings and she couldn't exactly admit them right now, either.

"We'll talk later," she promised.

He looked like he wanted to argue, but he released her and nodded. "I'll help Jim get the stuff inside. Go get ready."

Then he leaned in close to her ear and whispered, "You look absolutely breathtaking."

And then he eased by her on the steps and headed back down to the dock. Hannah's heart fluttered even more now.

He'd called her *sexy* multiple times, but he'd never used the word *breathtaking* and that was something else she'd need to process.

Was Will having stronger feelings for her, too? Would he admit it if he was? She knew his business and the label came first, so would he ever make time for more with her? What if this affair and all the recent changes she'd made in her life blew up in her face, and her label swap and career refresh were completely tarnished? She'd taken a risk by deciding to go in a new direction with her music and her producer at the same time. Had she sacrificed a predictable path for nothing?

There were too many questions that had her head spinning. By the time she made it back up to her bedroom, Hannah was ready for a nap instead of more photos.

"Care to tell me what's going on?"

Hallie stood in the middle of the room, holding on to the next outfit they'd chosen for the photos.

"What do you mean?" Hannah asked.

Hallie rolled her eyes. "You can't lie to me. What's going on with you and Will? I didn't miss the way you looked at him."

Hannah didn't want to lie to her sister and she hated the guilt that came along with all the sneaking. She also needed some sound advice.

Hannah crossed over to her vanity and sank down onto the plush stool. Hallie came up behind her and met her gaze in the mirror's reflection.

"We've been sleeping together."

Hallie's eyes widened. "Hannah!"

"I know, I know." She closed her eyes and sighed before meeting her sister's gaze again. "We were trying to keep everything separate, but..."

"Oh, no." Hallie came around and propped a hip on the edge of the vanity as she clutched the hanger with the clothes. "You're in love with him, aren't you?"

The burn in Hannah's throat and nose was all the warning she had before her eyes started filling. Damn it, she rarely cried, but lately she had zero control over her emotions.

"Oh, honey." Hallie crossed the room and laid the clothes on the bed before coming back and wrapping her arms around Hannah. "Does he know?"

Hannah sniffed, trying to blink away the tears. She was an ugly crier and she had a photo shoot to get back to. Her timing was so screwed lately—on everything from her emotions to her meltdowns.

"He has no idea," she admitted, easing back from her sister's shoulder. "I don't know what to do, but please don't say anything."

Hallie smiled. "That's a given."

Hannah shifted back toward the mirror and studied her reflection. "We're going to need to redo what the team did."

"Maybe I shouldn't have sent them away," Hallie laughed. "We can do this, though. Let's get through the shoot and then you can decide what to do about Will. I'll give advice or just listen. Whatever you need."

Hannah breathed a sigh of relief. "You took that much better than I thought you would."

Her sister's grin faltered. "Well, I really want to shake you and ask you what you were thinking, but he's hot and there's no going back in time, so we'll work with the present."

The present. Yes, that's what Hannah needed to

focus on. The shoot was happening now and there was nothing she could do about her newly discovered feelings in the next hour or so.

But once this was over, she was going to have to talk to Will and she had no idea what she should say.

Fifteen

"Care to tell me what's going on?"

Hannah sat next to Will in his SUV as he headed toward Mags's charity event. Something had been so off with her since the photo shoot a couple of days ago. He'd tried to pry it out of her, but she just said she was thinking and working on new material.

Artists in general were a moody bunch, but Will couldn't help wondering what else was bothering her. This silence and staring into space went well beyond being in a creative season.

Hannah reached over and grabbed his hand. "You keep asking me that and I promise, I'm fine. Just anxious for tonight."

"Because of Mags?"

"Because we're coming to this event together."

Will had been over this, but he'd tell her again.

"Even with our personal relationship aside, I would've come here with you to put up a united front, anyway. We want people and the press to associate you with Elite now. There's nothing more for anyone else to read in to it."

Except he was going to have a hell of a difficult time keeping his hands off her in the outfit she'd chosen. She was wearing a black double-breasted jacket dress. The damn thing stopped just beneath her ass and was cut low in the front, giving a sexy glimpse of the swell of her breasts. Of course, in true Hannah fashion, the entire jacket was outlined in black sequins to give off more sparkle. She'd paired the dress with black strappy sandals and had painted her toes in black glitter.

He couldn't wait to get back to his place and undo those four buttons and see what she was wearing underneath.

"Cash is planning on meeting us there," Will went on. "We'll all three work the cameras and then the two of you can mingle together."

Granted this night was about fundraising to help with the storm fund, but the press and media would be all over, just waiting to get an inside scoop. And just like everyone else attending the event, Will planned on using Mags's dime to get some free publicity.

When they pulled in front of Mags's house, there were cars everywhere and valets taking keys. Will assisted Hannah from the car then promptly released her hand. As much as he wanted to hold on to it or place his palm at the small of her back to escort her, he had to be doubly cautious tonight.

As they ascended the steps, he leaned over and whispered, "I'm going to strip you out of that dress the first chance I get."

Those wide, expressive eyes met his gaze and twinkled when they caught his crooked grin. He was ready to turn around and retrieve his car and forget this whole charity ball. He would donate a million dollars to whatever foundation needed help.

"You can't talk like that," she murmured.

Will chuckled at her gasp. "Oh, I'll do more than talk. Now let's get this night over with."

He gestured for her to go ahead of him, so Hannah gripped her clutch and started up the steps. As much as he tried to be a gentleman and look away, he couldn't stop his eyes from landing on those swaying hips. She had to have known this outfit would drive him out of his ever-loving mind.

Will couldn't wait to get her home.

Home. Since when did he want to take her home? Probably since he'd started thinking of her as more than his artist or his lover. He respected Hannah, he valued her opinion and he loved getting to know more about her—the real, private Hannah.

Things between them were more serious than he was ready to admit.

As they stepped into Mags's front entryway, there

was a sea of people dressed in black and white. Waitstaff mingled in the crowd with trays of drinks and bite-size treats. Folks laughed, chatted, and snapped selfies all while professionals with cameras couldn't get enough.

"Wow," Hannah murmured. "This is a great turnout."

A man who Will hadn't seen before approached them.

"Good evening," he said. "Welcome. Mags will be down shortly, but in the meantime, the silent auction is set up in the formal dining area. Please take your time and bid as much as you can."

He moved on and greeted more guests, and Will glanced toward the open doorway the man had labeled as the formal dining area.

"Want to check it out?" he asked.

Hannah nodded and started to follow him, only to be stopped by a journalist Will had dealt with many times before.

"Good evening, Josie," he greeted.

The petite redhead smiled. "Hey, Will. Would you mind if I snag a couple of photos of Hannah?"

"By all means." Will stepped aside. "Cash should be here soon, as well. You know they're gearing up for a big tour."

Hannah posed while Josie snapped away. "I heard that. I definitely want to get a few photos of them together."

"I'm here."

Will turned to see his brother wave as he wound through a group clustered at the front door.

"Perfect timing," Hannah told him. "Get on in here and make me look good."

Cash laughed. "Darlin', you couldn't look any better."

He kissed her on the cheek and slid an arm around her waist as they smiled for Josie.

Will remained on the side, trying like hell not to let his jealousy get the best of him. Cash had a natural charm and he and Hannah had become friends. Other than Cash stating the obvious about Hannah being gorgeous, his brother hadn't made a play for her. But still, Will didn't like another man's lips on her cheek or arm around her…even if that man was his brother.

Damn it. He didn't want to have deeper feelings for Hannah. They couldn't *afford* deeper feelings. There was too much at stake—her career, the tour, the awards ceremony tomorrow. Not to mention Cash's career.

"I hear you're both up for some big awards," Josie said. "Sounds like this tour is going to be a sellout."

Hannah glanced to Cash and shrugged. "I'd be fine with that."

"Do you have room for one more in this crowd?"

Will turned to see Eleanor glide into the room like the socialite diva she was. All elegance and grace with a bit of spitfire.

"Of course," Josie exclaimed. "This is wonderful."

"Gram, you look radiant."

No doubt. Eleanor slid between Cash and Hannah and simply beamed at the photographer.

"That's the whole point of these parties, yes? To shine."

Eleanor did just that as she smiled for the camera and shared laughs with Cash and Hannah. All too soon it wasn't just Josie taking photographs of the threesome. More of the exclusively invited media and even some guests were snapping their own pictures.

The clinking of a glass caught everyone's attention and the crowd started to quiet down. It didn't take long to see why.

"Thank you all for coming out tonight."

Will glanced up to the balcony stretching across the second story that overlooked the crowd below. Mags perched herself up there like a queen looking down on her peasants…and she was wearing bright, neon pink.

Of course, she wouldn't follow her own black-and-white rules. Mags's ego was too large to cater to stipulations…even her own.

"I hope we can raise an exorbitant amount of money for Beaumont Bay," she went on. "I love my beloved little town and hope to restore it and make it bigger and better than ever before."

"She's laying it on thick," Cash muttered to Will.

Mags never did anything halfway and she sure as hell never did anything without a flair for the dramatic. Will didn't understand how Hannah had stayed with Cheating Hearts for so long.

Once Mags finished her clearly rehearsed speech, she came down the curved staircase and joined the party. She was immediately handed a drink and Will tapped Cash's arm.

"Let's go into the dining room."

He turned to Hannah, but she was already heading that way. Looked like she wasn't ready to make small talk with Mags, either.

As soon as they entered, there were displays of various items, from guitars to autographs, from trips abroad to a brand-new yacht.

These items had all been donated by various folks both in and out of Beaumont Bay, all for the sake of rebuilding the town. Will couldn't believe what Mags had accomplished…or rather, what her assistant had accomplished. He doubted Mags did much more than tell her stylist what shade of pink she wanted for the event.

"Damn, that yacht is calling my name," Cash said as he picked up the pen to place his bid.

Will laughed. "You won't have time to enjoy it once you start touring."

"Sounds like I should outbid you."

Will turned to see Gavin with a leggy brunette on his arm. Will hadn't seen this woman before, but Gavin liked to date around and never let anything get too serious. He was too busy putting out fires and making his clients look good to give energy to a relationship.

"Glad you could join us," Cash stated. "But you won't outbid me."

"Has anyone bid on that trip to the Italian villa?" Luke came up beside them, sans date, with a big grin on his face. "Sorry I'm late. Had to handle an issue at Cheshire."

Will really didn't know what he wanted to bid on. It wasn't necessarily the prize that appealed to him, but rather giving back.

"You two duke it out over the trip and the yacht," Will told them. "I'm going over here to get this framed print of one of Willie's original lyrical notes."

"You've got to be kidding me," Hannah growled.

Will turned to see Hannah standing at the display of guitars. He crossed to her and started to reach for her…but caught himself just in time.

"What's wrong?" he asked.

She simply pointed. "That's mine. I left it at Cheating Hearts because she said she wanted to keep it hung in the lobby for decoration."

Will wasn't surprised Mags had lied. The woman was ruthless and did anything she wanted without worrying or caring who she pissed off.

"I'm so glad I'm out of there," Hannah added.

"Want me to bid on this for you?" Cash asked.

Will glared at his brother and Cash held his hands up. "Excuse me," Cash muttered.

"I'll get it," Will vowed.

"No, that's silly." Hannah shook her head. "I'm just ticked she lied to me. I would have donated anything to the auction had she simply asked."

"Excuse me, Ms. Banks."

Hannah leaned around Will to see who was requesting her and she instantly smiled. There was no hint that she'd just been upset or angry.

"I'm sorry to interrupt," the young man said. "My name is Alan and I'm new with *Country Life* magazine and I was hoping to get a few photos."

"Of course," she said, beaming. "Where would you like them?"

He shrugged. "It's so crowded in here. How about something toward the back of the house?"

"That would be fine." Hannah shot Will a look. "Don't bid on anything for me. I'll be right back."

Will watched her follow the man out the wide doorway and disappear around the corner.

"Something going on with you two?" Cash asked.

"What?" Will asked, noticing Gavin and Luke gathering in close like little old gossipy ladies. Gavin's date seemed to still be surveying the auction items.

"You and Hannah," Cash clarified. "What's going on?"

"I'm her new producer." Will hoped stating the obvious would work. "That's it."

"You seemed pretty territorial a minute ago." Cash crossed his arms over his chest. "I haven't seen you like that with any other artist of yours."

"Hannah isn't like other artists," he told Cash. "She's just come from Mags's label and is trying to grow her career in a new direction."

"That has nothing to do with you offering to get that guitar for her," Luke chimed in. "She can afford it if she wants it back."

Great, now he was on his brothers' radar. He seriously had to watch himself. He'd let his emotions overtake common sense a moment ago and that could prove to be a problem.

"Listen," he began as he shifted to face them all. "If something was going on, don't you think you all would know?"

Cash's lips quirked. "I'm pretty sure we all know now."

Will looked from Cash to Gavin to Luke and all three of them had that smug grin that said they knew.

Well, damn it.

Sixteen

"Let's try in here," Alan said.

Confused, Hannah stopped. They were outside a door and she had no clue what was on the other side.

"I thought we were doing something candid," she said.

"We are," he assured her. "Mags said I could use this room."

Something seemed off and she wasn't sure what. Even though there was a house full of people, that didn't mean a crazed fan hadn't gotten in, and now she was technically alone in a hallway with him.

"I'm not so sure," she told him. "How about we go into the foyer and get something on the steps or even me with a few of the other stars that are here."

The door opened and Mags stood there with a smirk. “Thank you, Alan. That will be all.”

The young man looked at Hannah like he wanted to apologize, but he ultimately nodded to Mags and walked away. Hannah didn’t like being set up.

“You could have just asked to talk to me,” Hannah said, still remaining in the hallway.

“We needed privacy,” Mags told her. “Come in.”

Hannah sighed. “I don’t have time for games and I’m not coming in. Now, if you’ll excuse me, I’m getting back to *your* party.”

Mags reached for Hannah’s arm before she could turn away. “Oh, you’ll want to hear what I have to say if you want to protect your man.”

Her man? A chill went down Hannah’s spine. What did Mags think she knew? Hannah and Will had been completely private. She hadn’t said a word and she knew Will hadn’t, either. Maybe Mags was just assuming or trying to trap Hannah.

Regardless of whatever Mags did or didn’t know, Hannah couldn’t just walk away. If she had something on Will, Hannah needed to know.

She took a step toward Mags, causing the woman to step back. When they were in the room, Mags closed the door and Hannah found herself in the library. She’d been to this house several times over the years for various parties and business meetings, but she hadn’t ever been in the library before.

Hannah didn’t bother looking around or taking in

anything. She really wanted Mags to get to the point so they could go back to the party.

"When you left Cheating Hearts, I assumed it was because you and I had a slight disagreement on your music."

Slight disagreement? More like Hannah was done being controlled, but she chose to remain silent.

"I had no idea you were sleeping with Will to get what you wanted."

Hannah laughed. "What on earth are you talking about? I'm not sleeping with anybody. I'm too busy, but thanks for your concern with my love life. If that's all—"

"Lying won't make this conversation end any sooner."

Mags went to the small ornate desk in the corner and pulled something from a drawer. When she came back, she handed Hannah some photographs.

"I have these," Mags stated. "And all I have to do is release them to any media outlet. I'm sure anyone would love to know your deepest secret."

Hannah looked at one photo after another. They were images of her and Will on his landing from the other night. When they'd been talking, then kissing, and when he'd lifted her into his arms.

Damn it. Mags had to have had someone following them with a hell of a camera that could catch these from such a distance.

"So what?" Hannah hoped her calm demeanor

would take the wind out of Mags's sails. "We're adults. We can do what we want in our spare time."

"Is that how the public will see it?" Mags countered. "Or will they think you are sleeping your way into a new chapter? Will they think Elite is dirtier than their squeaky-clean image portrays? How do you think this will look for your career or for Will's label?"

Fear started building within her and Hannah wanted to run from this room and go warn Will. Who knew if Mags would do anything with these photos—or maybe she already had?

"So what do you want?" Hannah asked. "I assume that's why you showed these to me. You want to blackmail me."

Mags's smile widened, her eyes sparkled. The damn woman was sneaky and she got off on making people miserable to get her way.

"You were my biggest star," Mags stated. "I want you to come back to Cheating Hearts."

Hannah waited for the rest or for Mags to say she was kidding, but the woman stood there, completely serious, and Hannah's stomach sank.

"I can't just return," she exclaimed. "I signed with Elite. I have started recording. I have a tour scheduled with Cash."

Mags waved a hand in the air as if Hannah was speaking nonsense. "All of that can be taken care of. I pay my lawyers a hefty sum."

No doubt her lawyers were crooked because

Gavin had always refused to work with Mags. Gavin might be ruthless, but that's because he studied the law and knew it inside and out. He could make things happen, but in a completely legal manner.

"Why would I come back to Cheating Hearts?" Hannah asked. "Because you have a few photos?"

"Because once I release these with an exclusive story that my number-one star confided in me her real reason for leaving, who do you think people will believe?" Mags asked. "You'll come along with some story after, but the damage to your name and to Will's name will already be out there. You'll just look like you're making excuses."

How could Hannah get out of this? Mags had her in a tough spot, but there was no way Hannah could let Will get hurt or put a black mark over Elite's reputation.

"Think about it and you can let me know in two days."

Hannah pulled in a deep breath. "How do I know you won't send those pictures out before then?"

Mags shrugged. "The same way I know you'll make the right decision."

Hannah didn't want to look at the conniving woman another second. She turned and let herself out of the room, then made her way back down the hallway. She ran in to Alan, whom she had to assume was the one who'd taken the scandalous pics. He wouldn't meet her gaze and Hannah wondered just how much he'd been paid for those images.

She finally found Will where he was standing with Cash in the ballroom on the other side of the house. By the time she found him, she wasn't shaking quite as much. But she still had that unsettling fear and worry.

How could she protect him? Was that even possible? Mags was right that if she hit the media first, her story would be more believable than anything Hannah or Will shared after.

So what if she and Will released the story first? That would completely remove the control and power from Mags. She wouldn't have a leg to stand on. Yes, Hannah had been wanting to keep their affair under wraps, but hadn't she just realized she loved Will?

She'd tell him how she felt, put it all on the line, and they'd go public. She had nothing left to lose.

Now was the time to write the story their own way. No more waiting.

She stepped between Will and Cash and pasted on a smile. "Did I miss anything?"

Will handed Hannah a glass of wine he'd apparently gotten for her. She could use it right about now.

"Just Gavin and Luke battling it out over some auction items and your gram smiling for pictures and schmoozing the crowd," Cash said, then his eyebrows drew in as he studied her. "You were gone a while. Did that guy get the pictures he needed?"

Hannah hated lying. She hated the guilt, but now was not the time to tell anyone what had happened—she wasn't even sure she'd ever tell anyone. But she was hoping to tell Will she loved him and that would solve everything. At least, she hoped.

"Oh, he got what he wanted."

No doubt a hefty pay from Mags for doing all her dirty work. Hannah really needed to process everything and figure out what to do next.

What if Will didn't feel the same way about her? What if he didn't want to go public?

What if Mags did get the one up on them?

"Look at this trio." Mags sidled up to them with two drinks in her hand. "I believe you need one of these, Mr. Sutherland."

She handed a drink to Cash and smiled. Hannah clutched her own glass and used every ounce of her willpower not to walk away. She had to remain strong, she had to somehow not let Mags win this fight. Hannah had finally gotten to a point where she might actually get to perform her own music. Will had been interested and he'd told her the songs were really good, but he hadn't yet committed. Surely, he would.

And surely he would respond to her confession of love with one of his own, or at least a willingness to see where this could go.

Alan came up with his camera, but wouldn't meet Hannah's eyes. "How about a shot of this group?"

"Perfect," Mags declared with a wide smile. "Let's gather in."

Thankfully Hannah was between Cash and Will and Mags had to stand on the other side of Cash.

This was one of those times when Hannah was glad she'd perfected her fake smile. She certainly wasn't feeling very festive right now.

"Perfect," Alan said as he glanced to his screen. "Thanks."

When he moved on, Mags turned to face them once again.

"I'm so glad you all could come. I assume you placed some bids."

"We did," Cash confirmed. "Hannah actually wants that guitar back."

It took everything in her not to ram her elbow into his side to shut him up.

Mags's eyes landed on Hannah. "Oh, darling, I assumed when you told me I could keep it, you wouldn't mind that I put it in the auction."

"I would have donated it had you asked," Hannah replied. "Assuming things can get you into trouble."

Mags's eyes narrowed for a fraction of a second before she shrugged and took a sip of her wine. "I'm not too worried about my assumptions. I tend to be right and everything works out as it should."

Mags turned her head and waved to someone across the room. "If you'll excuse me, I need to see some other guests and I simply must find time for a photo with Eleanor. Stay as long as you like and enjoy."

Yes, Hannah was sure Gram couldn't wait for that photo opportunity.

Once Mags was gone, Hannah was more than

ready to go. She'd had enough "fun" for one night and a headache was slowly settling in. She needed to talk to Will now, somewhere they wouldn't have an audience.

"What was all that about?" Will asked her.

"What?"

He shifted so he stood in front of her now. "Seemed like you and Mags were talking in code or something. Care to share?"

Hannah shook her head. "No code. She's just being her arrogant self."

Will didn't look like he believed her at all, but she wasn't about to say anything more. She drained her glass and placed it on a tray as a waiter walked by, then grabbed her clutch from beneath her arm.

"I'm getting a headache," she told Will. "Do you mind if we skip out? Or I can call a driver and you can stay."

He seemed to study her once again with that quizzical stare. Damn it, she loved him. He cared about her and Hannah truly believed he wanted what was best for her.

Nerves consumed her and she nearly felt ill from the worry of telling him her true feelings and asking him to go public. There was so much on the line… and her heart was the most important.

Will had to be on the same page so they could get to the media before Mags tarnished their names.

"Let's go," Will said, giving Cash his empty glass. "You're looking pale."

Yeah, and she suddenly felt sick to know that if Will didn't love her, if he didn't agree to take their relationship public, then Hannah would to have to hurt him to save him. She'd have to leave Will and Cheating Hearts and her dreams of her new look and sound behind.

"Do you want me to do anything?" Cash asked.

Will shook his head. "Just tell Gavin and Luke I'll see them later."

And with that, Will placed his arm on her elbow and escorted her out of the ballroom…but not before Hannah caught Mags flashing a smirk their way.

Seventeen

The car ride back to his house was completely silent. Will didn't press, but he knew something was wrong. He also didn't attempt to take her back to her place because he wanted to be alone with her… and that was before he realized something had happened at the party.

Now he had to figure out who the hell had upset Hannah, because she'd left for pictures and come back a totally different person. And she'd been lying when she'd said there was no secretive talk between her and Mags.

Likely Mags had gotten to Hannah, but what had the narcissist mogul said?

Once they were inside, Will reset the alarm and turned to Hannah.

"Talk."

Her eyes widened. "Excuse me?"

"Tell me what's gotten you so upset."

She blew out a sigh and rubbed her head. "I'm not upset, Will. But I have been thinking."

He crossed his arms over his chest and stared at her. "What about?"

"Us."

"Professionally or personally?"

She blinked and dropped her hands. "Both."

He said nothing because her tone and her stance told him nothing good was going to come from this conversation.

"I care about you, Will. More than I should and more than I wanted to, but there it is."

She cared for him? They hadn't planned on this, but part of him wanted her to tell him more. He wanted to know where she thought they should go or if she just wanted to get that off her chest. He needed more information.

But she went on.

"We need to go public with what's going on between us."

Will waited a second, wondering when the punchline came for this joke, but Hannah just continued to stare at him.

Then he laughed and shook his head. "What the hell are you talking about? What did Mags say to you?"

"Leave Mags out of it," Hannah demanded. "This is between you and me."

Confused, Will took another step forward. "She said something that upset you. Is she blackmailing you? Talk to me, Hannah."

The worried look in her eyes had him realizing just how concerned she was.

"I just think our relationship is moving in a new direction," she told him. "We went on a date, you surprised me with a picnic, and now you know I have feelings for you. Why shouldn't we go public? It would boost presales and we wouldn't always have to sneak around. Maybe we could go out in public for coffee or just a walk around the lake. Will, I know it's not what we've been doing, but I need this."

Something was off and he wasn't giving in until she told him what was going on. This all had to do with Mags—there wasn't a doubt in his mind.

"Hannah, you're in my every fantasy and it's clear I can't resist you, but, we can't go public right now," he informed her, afraid of all of this spiraling out of his control. "It's not a smart business move."

Her chin started to quiver, but she shook her head and glanced away. When she focused back on him, she'd composed herself and pulled in a breath. But he could see the pain in her eyes. Those bright eyes that once held so much fire and passion now hinted that she was on the verge of a breakdown.

"So you won't go public about our relationship?"

Will pulled in a deep breath. “No, I won’t. This is the best option in the long run.”

Now those beautiful eyes welled up with tears and she attempted to blink them away. Tried and failed.

“The best option for who?” she whispered. “If we can’t go public, then maybe we shouldn’t be taking our personal relationship any further.”

“What are you talking about?” he asked.

“All of this,” she murmured, waving her hands, blinking again. “Maybe we shouldn’t be together.”

“Why won’t you tell me what happened with Mags?”

“Because that’s irrelevant. I want to know how you feel about me, but knowing you won’t go public tells me all I need to know.”

Frustrated, he blew out a sigh. “It doesn’t tell you anything, Hannah. This is just not the right time.”

“Would there ever be a right time?” she cried. “Because I can’t be with Elite knowing what we’ve shared and knowing that you threw it all away because you were scared for anyone to find out. Working with you would be too difficult.”

Shock at her swift threat had him angrier than ever.

“So you’d throw away everything if I don’t go public?” he asked.

Her eyes closed and a lone tear slipped down her flushed cheek. What the hell was going on in that head of hers? Why this ultimatum? Why now?

Will couldn’t stand it another second. Whatever

she was facing had her more torn up than he'd first thought. Why wouldn't she open up to him?

He closed the space between them and framed her face, using the pad of his thumb to swipe away her tears.

"Talk to me," he murmured.

She shook her head and closed her eyes. "I need you, Will. Just for tonight. One last time."

One last time? Like hell.

Will lifted her off her feet and started carrying her up the stairs. Her shoes—first one, then the other—clunked down and fell back to the foyer. She looped her arms around his neck and rested her head against his shoulder.

So long as he could keep her here, protect her, slay her demons, he damn well would. He just had to know what the hell he was facing. Going public was her answer…but what the hell was the problem?

But right now, she wanted him for comfort. And he was more than willing to oblige. Tomorrow, he'd find out exactly what happened.

Will laid Hannah carefully onto his bed and stood over her. He stripped out of his suit and got more and more turned on as she watched him. Her eyes were still damp, but that fire was back. There was no way she wanted to break things off, not even if he couldn't do as she asked and go public right now. She wouldn't leave him when she could look at him with that much pent-up desire.

He reached down and unfastened her buttons,

pulling the tuxedo jacket wide. She had on no bra and a skimpy pair of black lace panties that he wasted no time in sliding down her legs.

Will eased up onto the bed and curled his fingers behind her thighs. She gripped his shoulders and kept her eyes locked on him. He could see much more than passion… There was trust in her gaze.

That pull on his heart tightened and more than ever he wanted to protect her. Not just as an artist under his label, but as a woman he'd fallen for.

This was not supposed to happen, but it did and he would have to deal with it. If he wasn't mistaken, she'd fallen for him, as well, but there was that nonsense about breaking all ties.

Not going to happen.

And going public wouldn't be smart at this early stage. Maybe they could keep everything under wraps and he could deal with Mags. He had to maintain control here, he had to make sure both he and Hannah were safe. He would do anything for her, no matter what.

"Keep those pretty eyes on me," he murmured as he joined their bodies.

Her fingertips dug into his shoulders as he set the pace. Her hips ground against his, her soft pants and sighs had him pushing harder, but her eyes never wavered from his.

What he'd thought would be gentle and soft turned to fire. Even though he loomed over her, Hannah set the rhythm.

She jerked faster as she locked her ankles behind his back and arched her body against his. Will let her take the lead and use him for whatever she needed. He realized he would do anything for her, no matter the cost.

When her body tightened all around him, she still kept her gaze on him, and Will let himself go. He stared into her eyes a second before easing down to capture her lips. He wanted her to feel his passion, his love. He wanted her to realize that he wasn't letting her go without a fight, but she had to reconsider going public.

"Stay," he told her after as he gathered her close. "Tomorrow's problems will come soon enough."

She didn't say a word, but right before he drifted off to sleep, he felt a warm tear on his side. Will held her tighter and vowed to find out what she was dealing with and take care of it. Never again on his watch would someone hurt her.

"Well, well, well. To what do I owe this pleasure?"

Will stood on Mags's doorstep much too early in the morning. He'd left Hannah sleeping with a note on his pillow that he would be right back.

"We need to talk." He brushed past her and let himself in. "What the hell did you tell Hannah last night?"

Mags closed the door and turned to face him, feigning shock. "What are you talking about?"

"I'm not here to play games, just tell me what the hell happened? You're holding something over her."

"If you two are having a lovers' quarrel, that has nothing to do with me," she sneered.

Ah, so that was it. Mags had somehow discovered he and Hannah were lovers.

"You blackmailed her," Will stated. "With what?"

"What did she tell you?"

Will was about done with this nonsense. He clenched his fists at his sides and ground his teeth.

"What. Did. You. Do?"

Mags shrugged. "I merely showed her some interesting photographs of the two of you."

He wasn't going to ask about the pictures or how she'd gotten them. That wasn't the point right now.

"So what?" he countered. "A few pictures wouldn't be anything to hold over her."

Mag smirked. "No, but giving them to the media would. What would her fans think? What would your other artists think if they saw these photos? Would they think she went to Elite to sleep her way into the next chapter of her career?"

Rage pumped through him, but he said nothing as everything hit him at once. Hannah's threat to leave was her way of trying to protect him and likely trying to protect his label. She'd been willing to throw it all away so his name wasn't pulled through the mud.

That was the love she'd been talking about.

"Imagine if I accidentally let those pictures slip into the wrong hands. What headlines would be posted?" Mags went on. "Damning for her career and your label. Such a shame, too."

"You won't get away with this."

"No? Did she already break things off with you? I gave her two days to think about it. Looks like she moved fast."

Will was raised to respect women, but right now, he had nothing but disdain for Mags Dumond.

"Whatever you think you can pull here, you're wrong," he warned. "You crossed the line this time and Hannah will not be coming back to Cheating Hearts."

"No?" Mags asked, her eyebrows raised. "Seems if she broke things off with you, she's already made her decision."

Will was done here. He was done with her attitude, he was done with the games, and he was done with letting anyone threaten Hannah.

He let himself out and headed back to his car.

The awards ceremony was tonight, and Mags would be there, too. Will had to make sure Hannah steered clear of Mags. He would enlist the help of his brothers and explain everything that was going on.

Hannah wanted them to go public. Well, she hadn't seen public yet.

As soon as he got into his SUV, he dialed up Cash, but got no answer. Then he tried Gavin, again with no answer. Strange. He called Luke and finally got him to pick up.

Once Will explained everything, Luke agreed to

help and have his back. Luke wasn't actually part of the country music world, but he always went to the ceremonies, to network and support his brothers. The Sutherlands were a team, like a wolf pack. All the more reason Mags should watch the hell out.

Nobody was getting to Hannah.

Eighteen

Hannah had slipped out of Will's house while he had been gone. She had no idea where he went, but she needed to get out. She'd slept with him last night, because she'd needed one last time before exiting his life for good. Saying goodbye face-to-face would have been too difficult this morning after sleeping in his arms all night, so she was actually thankful he wasn't there.

His note hadn't indicated where he'd gone, just that he would be back soon and he'd see her then. Hannah grabbed a pen and jotted her own note on the other side, that she'd see him at the awards ceremony that evening.

Hannah had called Hallie to come give her a ride back home and confessed everything to her sister.

She'd needed to purge her feelings and nobody was better at giving advice than her twin. Now they were attempting to get ready for the awards show and Hannah would much rather stay home.

"If you love him, tell him again," Hallie insisted as she sprayed her hair. "Maybe he just needed a little time. Maybe he feels the same."

Hannah fastened her strappy heels and came to her feet, smoothing down her dark blue gown. She loved this dress, loved her look for the evening, but she just wasn't feeling it like she normally did. Everything had changed and she would never be the same, no matter what happened with Will and Mags. Her heart had been broken when Will had said no to going public. It'd been like he was saying no to what they could have together. There was no going back from something like that.

"I'm not telling him that I love him again." Hannah grabbed her clutch and tossed her cell and lip gloss inside. "I put my heart on the line once already for him."

Hallie opened her mouth and started to say something, but Hannah held up her hands. "End of discussion. Now, are we ready to go? The car should be here."

Hallie ultimately nodded, though Hannah knew her sister wanted to say much more. Hannah couldn't keep up this back-and-forth. As much as she wanted to confess everything to Will, she also knew Mags would follow through with her threat.

That woman would do anything to have Hannah back and make Will suffer. She'd always been a jealous creature. First, she'd been jealous of Eleanor years ago, then she'd been jealous of Hannah's fame when Hannah wanted to branch out and do her own lyrics, and now she was jealous of Will for signing Hannah.

Well, now Mags might just get her way because Hannah couldn't stay with Elite and be the reason their reputation was torn to shreds. And while Will was angry now, he'd come to see that this was better in the long run. Or maybe he wouldn't, because Hannah was never going to tell him what happened.

Thankfully Hallie didn't bring up the whole *L* word again as they rode to the venue for the ceremony. As soon as the car came to a stop, the back door opened and the paparazzi were all in their faces snapping pics and calling Hannah's name.

"I'll stay behind," Hallie told her.

Hannah grabbed her sister's hand. "No, you won't. You're right here with me and just as important."

Hallie smiled and nodded, squeezing her hand in return.

They posed and laughed, and Hannah answered a few questions along the way. Everyone wanted to know where Cash was, but she assumed he'd be along anytime if he hadn't passed through already. In a perfect world, they would have had to start doing public events together…but that perfect world was now shattered thanks to some overpaid photographer and Mags's evil streak.

"How about that upcoming tour with Cash?" one journalist called out.

Hannah smiled. "Nothing is finalized quite yet."

She didn't want to lie, but she also couldn't come out and answer the question. Everyone would know soon enough that all of those plans were no more.

Hannah and Hallie moved across the carpet and into the venue, where the majority of stars and guests were already seated. Hannah finally breathed a sigh of relief once she was beyond the questions and flashing bulbs. She hadn't thought about how to answer the questions about her tour or her new album.

Nerves tightened in her belly that had nothing to do with her upcoming nomination for Entertainer of the Year. This entire mess had snowballed into lies and broken hearts, and it was going to get much worse before it would get better. But in the long run, Will's label would remain untarnished and so would his name. That's all that mattered to her right now.

He might not love her, but she wasn't sure if she'd ever stop loving him.

Hannah was escorted to her seat and she wasn't at all surprised to see she was in the front row, right next to all the Sutherland brothers.

Wait. Where was Cash? The show was getting ready to start and he wasn't here yet?

Will met her eyes, but then that stare traveled down her body and she knew he loved the dress.

She'd shown him a couple of options a few days ago and he'd told her how gorgeous she'd look in blue and how he couldn't wait to see it on his bedroom floor.

"Cash running late?" she asked, shaking off the image of what would never be.

Their grim faces had her easing into her seat and leaning over. "What happened?"

"He got arrested after the party last night," Gavin whispered.

Shock filled her. "What on earth for? What happened?"

"DUI."

Confused, Hannah looked to Will. "I only saw him with one drink."

"Yeah, that's the issue," Gavin added. "He wasn't drunk. I'm taking care of things."

The music started up, indicating the show was beginning, and Hannah sat there in utter disbelief. What was going on? Cash might sing about drinking and having that good ol' country boy life, but she'd never seen him drunk and he certainly hadn't been last night when she'd left.

As the ceremony went on, Hannah had a difficult time focusing due to her worry about Cash. Not to mention her anxiety over having Will sitting just two seats down from her. At least Hallie was at her side. She needed her sister now more than ever.

When Eleanor glided onto the stage in a fitted red beaded gown, the crowd cheered and clapped. Hannah couldn't help but smile and feel slightly calmer.

"It is my honor and privilege to present the final award tonight, for Entertainer of the Year."

Hallie reached for Hannah's hand and squeezed. Right now, Hannah didn't care much about the award, she just wanted to settle this roller coaster with Will and find out what happened to Cash. A DUI made absolutely no sense whatsoever. Not to mention he lived at the lake where the party had been held. Who the hell was trying to get Cash into trouble? Something was off here.

Eleanor went through the nominees and Hannah didn't miss the camera in her face to catch her reaction as her gram read Hannah's name as the winner. Eleanor met her gaze and beamed a huge smile as she clapped.

Hallie jumped up with Hannah and gave her a hug, then Hannah turned to Gavin and Luke, who patted her on the back and congratulated her. Will's smile widened as he nodded his congrats. She wished she could celebrate this moment with him, fling herself into his arms and not have to hide her feelings. Unfortunately, that was impossible.

Hannah climbed the stairs to the stage and reached for the award.

Gram gave her a big hug and whispered in her ear, "There's another surprise coming."

Confused, Hannah pulled back, but her gram stepped away from the mic to give Hannah the space for her speech. She hadn't brought up a note or anything. Winning hadn't even crossed her mind because she'd been so worried about everything else going on. So she just decided to speak from her heart.

"This is such an honor," Hannah began. "I value this award so much considering it's voted on by the fans. I love my job and each of you. Being a performer has always been a dream of mine, so thank you for letting me live my dream."

The audience clapped, but then she realized she wasn't standing at the mic alone. She glanced over and Will stood at her side. She covered the mic with one hand while holding her award with the other.

"What are you doing?" she whispered as her heart thumped harder and her stomach twisted into knots.

All Will did was smile and reach for her hand that covered the mic. He didn't let go and Hannah had no clue what was happening, but he eased his arm around her waist and leaned into the stand.

"Good evening, everyone," he said. "Can we get another round of applause for this amazingly talented artist?"

Everyone cheered and Hannah smiled at the crowd, then turned to glance at Gram, who was still beaming like she knew some secret. Whatever was going on, Eleanor Banks and Will Sutherland had cooked up something.

The crowd's roar died down and Will kept his hold on her.

"Hannah recently signed with Elite Records and I'm thrilled to have her on my team," he went on.

"But the more I got to know her, the more I realized I wanted her on another team of mine."

Hannah jerked her attention to him when he released her and reached into his pocket as he got down on one knee. Hannah gasped.

"Will," she muttered. "What are you doing?"

He smiled. "I want you in my life, Hannah. I want to do everything together with you, in business and personally."

"You can't—"

He opened the ring box and Hannah gasped once again. What was he thinking? They couldn't do this…could they?

"I can," he retorted. "Marry me, Hannah. We'll tackle the world together."

Hannah couldn't stop the tears from forming. She leaned down, away from the mic.

"What about Mags?" she whispered.

"Nothing to worry about if we're making a formal announcement now, is there?" he asked, then came to his feet and pulled her in close to murmur in her ear. "And I'm not doing this because of her. I'm sorry I didn't respond sooner and that I made you worry. I love you, Hannah. I know you love me. Say yes."

She wrapped her arms around him and the crowd went wild. She couldn't hold back the tears as she nodded against his shoulder.

"Yes, yes, yes."

Will eased back, swiped the tears from her cheeks and pulled the ring from the box. He slid it perfectly onto her finger before holding her hand up for all to see.

The applause continued and Hannah could see her sister in the front row crying and taking a handkerchief from Gavin. Hannah couldn't believe this moment was happening, but she was so thrilled and totally in love with this man.

"Looks like I have more than a tour to plan for," Hannah announced into the mic.

Will reached around and kissed her. "I love you," he murmured again.

"I love you."

Will kissed her again and Hannah knew they were going to be an unstoppable team that nobody could mess with again.

Epilogue

"That was absolutely perfect."

Hannah stepped back from the mic and smiled as she met Will's gaze in the control room. She'd never felt more alive with her music than right at this moment recording her first track of her very own lyrics.

And there was her fiancée staring back at her with pride in his eyes. She never imagined her life would ever turn out this amazing.

"That's a wrap for today, Hannah."

She removed her earpiece and sat it on the stool before leaving the recording room and going in to see Will and the sound director.

"That really was amazing, Hannah," the sound

director told her. “I’ll get out of your way and see you Friday.”

“Thank you so much,” she told him. “I’m really excited for this project.”

“It’s going to be your best yet,” Will assured her.

Once they were alone, Will reached for her hands and pulled her closer.

“I cannot wait for your fans to hear this,” he told her, gliding his thumbs over the back of her hands. “I’m so glad you held on to that book of your music until you came to me.”

“Mags didn’t deserve them. She’ll really hate when she realizes these are all mine.”

Will laughed. “She’s still pissed she didn’t ruin us. She’ll breathe fire and have to make face for the public to save her reputation once she realizes just how far you and I are going with your new music.”

Hannah wrapped her arms around his neck and touched her lips to his briefly before easing back.

“Do you think she’ll retaliate?” Hannah asked. “I mean, she was so upset when I switched labels and had Cash framed for a DUI.”

The party last month at Mags’s house had resulted in Cash getting arrested on a bogus charge that Gavin quickly found out was absurd. They couldn’t exactly pinpoint Mags, but there was nobody else who would have done that…or anybody else who had the police in their pockets.

“I don’t care what she does,” Will told her. “We’re

together, your music is going to break chart records, and we're getting married. Nothing can stop us."

Hannah threaded her fingers through his hair and smiled. "You're right. Nothing can stop us."

And then she kissed him.

* * * * *

Dynasties: Beaumont Bay
What happens in Beaumont Bay
stays in Beaumont Bay.
This is the bedroom community where
Nashville comes to play!

Twin Games in Music City
by Jules Bennett—available now

Second Chance Country
by Jessica Lemmon—available May 2021

Kiss Me Again, Country
by Jules Bennett—available June 2021

Good Twin Gone Country
by Jessica Lemmon—available July 2021

COMING NEXT MONTH FROM

Available May 11, 2021

#2803 THE TROUBLE WITH BAD BOYS
Texas Cattleman's Club: Heir Apparent
by Katherine Garbera

Landing bad boy influencer Zach Benning to promote Royal's biggest soiree is a highlight for hardworking Lila Jones. And the event's marketing isn't all that's made over! Lila's sexy new look sets their relationship on fire... Will it burn hot enough to last?

#2804 SECOND CHANCE COUNTRY
Dynasties: Beaumont Bay • by Jessica Lemmon

Country music star Cash Sutherland hasn't seen Presley Cole since he broke her heart. Now a journalist, she's back in his life and determined to get answers he doesn't want to give. Will their renewed passion distract her from the truth?

#2805 SEDUCTION, SOUTHERN STYLE
Sweet Tea and Scandal • by Cat Schield

When Sienna Burns gets close to CEO Ethan Watts to help her adopted sister, she's disarmed by his Southern charm, sex appeal...and insistence on questioning her intentions. Now their explosive chemistry has created divided loyalties that may derail all her plans...

#2806 THE LAST LITTLE SECRET
Sin City Secrets • by Zuri Day

It's strictly business when real estate developer Nick Breedlove hires interior designer—and former lover—Samantha Price for his new project. Sparks fly again, but Samantha is hiding a secret. And when he learns the truth about her son, she may lose him forever...

#2807 THE REBEL HEIR
by Niobia Bryant

Handsome restaurant heir Coleman Cress has always been rebellious—in business and in relationships. Sharing a secret no-strings affair with confident Cress family chef Jillian Rossi is no different. But when lust becomes something more, can their relationship survive meddling exes and family drama?

#2808 HOLLYWOOD EX FACTOR
LA Women • by Sheri WhiteFeather

Security specialist Zeke Mitchell was never interested in the spotlight. When his wife, Margot Jensen, returns to acting, their marriage ends...but the attraction doesn't. As things heat up, are the problems of their past too big to overlook?

Country music star Cash Sutherland hasn't seen Presley Cole since he broke her heart. Now a journalist, she's back in his life and determined to get answers he doesn't want to give. Will their renewed passion distract her from the truth?

Read on for a sneak peek at
Second Chance Love Song
by Jessica Lemmon.

"Did you expect me to sleep in here with you?"

And there it was. The line that he hadn't thought to draw but now was obvious he'd need to draw.

He eased back on the bed, shoved a pillow behind his back and curled her into his side. Arranging the blankets over both of them, he leaned over and kissed her wild hair, smiling against it when he thought about the tangles she'd have to comb out later. He hoped she thought of why they were there when she did.

"We should talk about that, yeah?" he asked rhetorically. He felt her stiffen in his arms. "I want you here, Pres. In this bed. Naked in my arms. I want you on my dock, driving me wild in that tiny pink bikini. But we should be clear about what this is…and what it's not."

She shifted and looked up at him, her blue eyes wide and innocent, her lips pursed gently. "What it's not."

"Yeah, honey," he continued, gentler than before. "What it's not."

"You mean…" She licked those pink lips and rested a hand tenderly on his chest. "You mean you aren't going to marry me and make an honest woman out of me after that?"

Cash's face broadcasted myriad emotions. From what Presley could see, they ranged from regret to nervousness to confusion and finally to what she could only describe as "oh, shit." That was when she decided to let him off the hook.

Chuckling, she shoved away from him, still holding the sheet to her chest. "God, your face! I'm kidding. Cash, honestly."

He blinked, held that confused expression a few moments longer and then gave her a very unsure half smile. "I knew that."

"I'm not the girl you left at Florida State," she told him. "I grew up, too, you know. I learned how the world worked. I experienced life beyond the bubble I lived in."

She took his hand and laced their fingers together. She still cared about him, so much. After that, she cared more than before. But she also wasn't so foolish to believe that sex—even earth-shattering sex—had the power to change the past. The past was him promising to wait for her and then leaving and never looking back.

"That was really fun," she continued. "I had a great time. You looked like you had a great time. I'm looking forward to doing it again if you're up to the task."

Don't miss what happens next in…
Second Chance Love Song
by Jessica Lemmon, the second book in the Dynasties: Beaumont Bay series!

Available May 2021 wherever Harlequin Desire books and ebooks are sold.

Harlequin.com

HDEXP0421